"Well, well,"

"Afraid so," M

"I'd rather leave it wide open. I got friends outside watchin' just to make sure you don't try to frame me."

"I don't have to 'frame' you, Nick. You're going to put your head in your own noose before very long. You always have."

Nick's smile died. "Speak your piece, Dillon."

"All right. I don't want you to attend Abe's funeral. Abe disinherited you and your mother long ago. Besides that, I'm sure that you weren't invited by James and Jessica. I'll be watching you every minute. If you so much as sneeze wrong, I'll come down on you like a mountainside."

Nick snorted derisively. "You and your deputy ain't got nothin' on me and you never will." He dug into his pockets and flung money on the floor. "Here, Deputy Haggen. Buy yourself a bath, a shave, and a clean shirt. You're a disgrace to Dodge City."

Festus started for Nick, but Matt held him until the door shut. "Easy, Festus."

"I'd like to have a piece of him."

"We *all* would," Matt said. "And you can bet that, sooner or later, we all will."

Berkley Boulevard titles by Gary McCarthy

GUNSMOKE
GUNSMOKE: DEAD MAN'S WITNESS

GUNSMOKE™
DEAD MAN'S WITNESS

A NOVEL BY
GARY McCARTHY

*Based on the radio and television series
created by John Meston*

BERKLEY BOULEVARD BOOKS, NEW YORK

GUNSMOKE: DEAD MAN'S WITNESS

A Berkley Boulevard Book / published by arrangement with
Viacom Consumer Products, Inc.

PRINTING HISTORY
Berkley Boulevard edition / March 1999

The Penguin Putnam Inc. World Wide Web site address is
http://www.penguinputnam.com

ISBN: 0-425-16775-5

BERKLEY BOULEVARD
Berkley Boulevard Books are published by
The Berkley Publishing Group,
a member of Penguin Putnam Inc.,
375 Hudson Street, New York, New York 10014.
BERKLEY BOULEVARD and its logo
are trademarks belonging to Berkley Publishing Corporation.

PRINTED IN THE UNITED STATES OF AMERICA

10 9 8 7 6 5 4 3 2 1

GUNSMOKE™

DEAD MAN'S WITNESS

CHAPTER

1

One by one the collection of distinguished Dodge City founders and pioneers solemnly filed into the dim room until all five were gathered around the wasted but still imposing figure of Abraham Dawson. His eyes were closed and they at first thought he might already be dead, but then he suddenly began to cough. It was a tortured, hacking cough that racked the old cattleman's once impressive frame and left him pale, shaking, and struggling for breath. Young James Dawson and his twin sister, Jessica, both hurried to their father's side, each trying to give him help and a spittoon. When Abraham hawked up spittle, it was dark red.

The five men shifted uneasily. One of them, Bill Varner, the owner of the second largest cattle ranch and Abraham's longtime friend, said to the others, "I think it might be best if we returned some other time when Abe is feeling a little stronger."

"No," the dying man choked. "There might not be any time left in me."

There was no one willing to argue the point. In fact, all five were so shocked and appalled by their friend's emaciated appearance that they hardly knew what to say or do.

"Jessica, open the drapes a little and give me some daylight. I'm going to see the darkness soon enough."

Jessica pulled open the heavy velvet drapes and sunlight slanted through the bedroom window. Now it could be seen that this was an enormous room and that the old man lay on a stout four-poster bed. There were bookshelves lining most of the walls and the room was cluttered with saddles, bronze statues, and cowboy art. On one wall hung a gilt-edged proclamation from the mayor of Dodge City, proclaiming Abraham honorary mayor and most distinguished citizen of Kansas.

No one had to tell this collection of visitors what a sterling contribution to Kansas and Dodge City Abraham Marcus Dawson had made in his lifetime. He had tamed this land, wrested it from the Indians and then the buffalo bone pickers, and created a cattle empire second to none. In his later years, ashamed of his treatment of the Indians, he had become their staunchest advocate and most generous benefactor. The man could have been governor or a senator had he chosen, but politics had never been his forte, so he'd stayed on the land and molded a ranching dynasty and a reputation built on his word and handshake.

"Gentlemen," Abraham said, "I know how busy you all are and I want to begin by saying how much I appreciate your attendance and . . . far more, your long and loyal friendship."

"We're the ones that ought to be thanking you," Mr. Paulson, a retired minister and community leader, said. "Abe, isn't there anything that can be done?"

"No. Doc Adams says I've got a cancer in my lungs. I thought it was consumption, but he says not. Maybe it was all those Mexican cigars I smoked over the years that finally done me in. Dunno, and it don't much matter anymore. What does matter is that you are here and now I can say my final piece before cashing in."

Jessica bit her lower lip and tried not to cry. She didn't want to embarrass her father or make him ashamed. She glanced sideways at her brother, hoping that he would also be able to control his emotions. Although they were both seventeen, James was the one more devastated by the impending loss of their father. He and Abraham had been inseparable for years, and now, all too soon, he was the one that would have to run the Dawson Ranch with its crushing responsibilities. Thank God for their longtime foreman and friend, Hannibal, who had just entered the room with his hat in his rough old hands. Hannibal would guide James, but Jessica knew that her brother would need a lot of support, especially during this time of grieving.

"What I want to tell all of you is that I have just learned that my eldest son, Nick, is about to be released from prison."

The five men exchanged glances but said nothing.

"I know that this news comes as a shock," Abraham continued, "and I want you to understand that I had nothing to do with his being paroled years early. I have no idea how he managed to get out so early and I don't care. Nick is . . . is a great disappointment. He is his mother's son, not mine, and I have asked you here to

3

bear witness to the fact that I am disinheriting Nick . . . completely.''

Abraham looked to James and Jessica and the lines in his rugged and ravaged face softened. ''As you know, these are my beloved children born of my second wife— God rest her dear departed soul. Had it not been for James and Jessica, I think I might have lost heart and died soon after their mother. But I did not and life has been good these past eight years. Until . . . well, this illness.''

''You've been the best friend I ever had,'' choked the retired Homer T. Blasdell, one of Kansas's most respected circuit judges. ''I'll never forget that time you saved me from being lynched. You fought your way through that drunken bunch and brought law and order long before we had Marshal Matt Dillon, Chester, or Festus Haggen for protection.''

''No,'' Abraham said, ''you are the one that wielded the gavel and brought law to this territory. I didn't always agree with your courtroom decisions, but I always knew that they were based on law, without regard to the color of a man's skin or the size of his bank account. If you'd have been lynched, we'd have lost more than honor.''

Abraham looked at Forbes Montgomery, ever elegant and formal. ''Forbes, you were the one that loaned me the seed money to buy this ranch when I had little more than a pledge to repay you.''

''I've always been able to read men,'' Forbes replied with a trembling smile, ''and I knew that my money was safe and that it would grow. And, in those hard, early years, you came to me first for help, which I considered a privilege. Abraham, I . . .''

4

"It's all right," Abraham said, raising his hand. "You don't have to say anything. Your friendship speaks for itself. Hannibal, what can I say but thanks for being the best foreman in Kansas."

"My pleasure," Hannibal said, Adam's apple bobbing painfully up and down in his constricted throat. "You know I been proud to be of service. And don't worry about James, he'll do jest fine."

"Of course he will," Abraham said. "But he's going to need your help and guidance. In fact, he's going to need the help of each and every one of you dear friends. Will you give it to him?"

To the man they nodded their heads.

"Don't worry," the banker vowed. "His credit is as good as gold."

"And I'll see that young James stays to the righteous path," the former minister promised.

Austin Sinclair, a wealthy mining engineer from Colorado and a member of every civic group in Dodge City as well as its town council, was the quietest of them all, and so he just nodded to show that he would do anything necessary.

"Don't forget Jessica," Abraham said with a wink at his daughter. "She's got more of me in her than either of us would care to admit."

It was a joke and it brought a round of smiles.

"Abraham, I'll serve as legal counsel to them until they find a younger, better mind," Montgomery pledged.

"Good," the old rancher said, clenching his big fists. "And I want you to know that there will be some who will say I was wrong to cut my eldest son, Nick, out of all my inheritance."

"I wouldn't worry about that," the judge said. "Nick has a pretty bad reputation in these parts, notwithstanding your family name. I'm sorry, Abe, but you know that's the truth."

"I do," Abraham admitted. "And as you all know, he is not of my flesh and blood. I married his mother not realizing that she was with another man's child. I doubt it would have made any difference to me at the time because I was young, hot-blooded, and foolish. Flora was the most beautiful and spirited woman I'd ever seen and also the most cunning and devious, though I didn't see it way back then. I thought I could change her bad ways and raise her Nick as if he were my own. But I couldn't and maybe I'm to blame."

"Father," Jessica protested, "you treated us all the same. You never played favorites. Nick was given everything."

"That's true, my dear. And early on I could see that he was bad to the bone. I'll never forgive myself for the way he tormented you and James during your early years whenever my back was turned. Flora could have controlled the boy, but she was just as bad . . . worse, maybe. But that is all sad history and—"

Abraham broke out in another coughing fit. This time it was so violent that some of his old friends had to step out of the room because they could not bear to see him suffer and lose so much blood from his ravaged and failing lungs. Finally, mercifully, the coughing ended and Jessica motioned them back into the bedroom.

"He insists on finishing," she said. "Please, I know this is hard."

"What about you and James?" the minister asked.

"I'm sure that we need to talk to the Lord about His each and every day."

"Of course," she said as they regrouped around Abraham's bed. "Father, please try to keep this short. Your strength is not good."

"I know. I know. What I have left to say is this: With Hannibal's and God's help, there is no reason why anything need change on the Dawson Ranch. I addressed my men last week and told them the same thing. But I am worried about Nick and what he might do when he discovers that he is out of my will."

"Marshal Dillon can handle Nick," the judge said.

"I'm sure that he can," Abraham replied, "but Nick is smart. He won't go near Dodge City if he thinks Matthew might warn or even arrest him. Nick will come to this ranch and he might even bring some of his murderous friends."

"We'll make sure that he never gets past the gates," Hannibal promised. "We've got the men to stop him."

"I hope so," Abraham said, closely studying each and every one of his friends for what he knew would be the last time. "Because we all know that if Nick somehow found a way to gain control of the Dawson Ranch, he would use the resources I have amassed to quickly destroy anyone who opposed him. He would become a scourge upon this range, stealing cattle and preying on the smaller ranchers and farmers like a wolf among sheep."

"Abe, maybe you're exaggerating just a bit," Montgomery suggested. "I know Nick is dangerous and smart but—"

"Whoa," Abraham whispered. "He's far more than that. He's as cunning as a coyote and as deadly as a rattlesnake. Even more, when he discovers what I've done, he's going to blame James and Jessica, and so I fear for their lives."

"I can handle Nick," James said. "I'm finally big enough to whip him. And I'm the best pistol shot on this ranch."

"Son, I know you are brave and tough, but Nick has the edge in experience. He is also quick and would not hesitate an instant to put a bullet in your belly if he thought he could escape being arrested by Matt and hanged."

"Don't worry," Hannibal said, "we won't let him get near either Jim or Jessica."

"You can't keep them on this ranch forever," Abraham said. "Sooner or later there will be a showdown, if Nick doesn't kill someone else first and is hanged or returned to prison for life."

"Let's hope he just decides to stay away," Varner said. "Marshal Dillon roughed him up pretty good the last time they met, and Nick knows that he is a marked man if he returns to Dodge City."

"Matt can't arrest him for no reason," the judge said. "And I doubt that Nick would provoke the marshal or Festus under any circumstances. He's far too smart to do something that stupid."

"So what can be done, then?" Forbes Montgomery asked with a hint of exasperation.

"Nothing," Abraham told them. "And that is the problem. I will be dead and unable to protect my son and daughter, and so I'm asking for your help . . . in whatever way it might someday be needed if my worst fears come to pass and Nick seeks revenge."

"You have our words on that," Austin Sinclair told

him. "I say that knowing we are of one mind and one heart on this matter."

"Thank you!" Abraham said. "That is all that I wanted to know. Now, Jessica, will you go get the brandy and glasses? I think one final small celebration among old and dear friends is in order."

"Yes, Father."

"James?"

"Yes, sir?"

"Stay and drink with us. You're a man now and a man could find no better company than these gathered at my side."

James didn't trust himself to speak. But the tall, slender young rancher did manage to nod his head and keep his eyes from filling with tears.

CHAPTER

2

Matt was having a pretty good week, considering that most of the Texas cowboys were still in town celebrating in preparation for their long return trip south. He was taking the day off and going fishing with Doc and that was always one of his favorite pastimes. Matt heard that they were really biting down at the river and Doc had a few prime fishing holes in mind that he swore were loaded with pan-sized fryers. Doc was delightful company and an excellent fisherman and Matt also enjoyed the crusty old physician's dry wit and humor.

"I sure do wish I was a-goin' fishin' today with you," Festus whined, his boots up on his scarred old desk, his eyes sad and wistful. "I expect that at least you're goin' to have a nice day."

"Well, Festus, you had yesterday off. Why didn't you go fishing if that sounds so good?"

"I had other things to do."

Matt studied his deputy closely. "Such as?"

"Well, I was kept busy," Festus said, avoiding eye contact. "You know how it goes sometimes on your day off. One danged thing and then another keep comin' up all the time till, the first thing you know, the day is shot. Just gone!"

To emphasize his point, Festus snapped his fingers. "And I was kinder tired by yesterday afternoon, so I decided to lay down and rest my eyes a mite. First thing I know, it was evenin' and too late to go fishin'."

"Well," Matt said, "I'm sorry about that, but I suggest you plan your next day off a little bit more carefully. I try to get my outside chores all done and wipe the slate clean so that I'm completely free on my days off. Otherwise, you can wind up feeling you never have any fun."

"Matthew, that's real good advice," Festus agreed. "But I have a lot of extry outside responsibilities that you just don't have to worry about."

"Such as?"

"Well, I got to visit Mrs. Clancy. You know, I stop by just to make sure that the sweet old gal is all right and everything."

"You stop by to eat her pies and cookies, Festus."

Festus bristled. "Well, shoot, Matthew! You don't expect me to hurt her feelin's and turn her offer down, do you?"

"I guess not."

Matt was looking for his fishing pole and decided it was over at the boardinghouse where he was staying. At least, he hoped it was.

"And I also been a-lookin' in on that poor little widow woman, Mrs. Jensen. She is feelin' kinda down

12

since her husband accidentally shot hisself cleanin' that shotgun. Mrs. Jensen needs a little help now and then around the place and I just feel like helpin' her out is the neighborly thing to do."

"Mrs. Jensen gave you your last shave and haircut, didn't she? And mended that shirt and your stockings?"

"Well, what has that got to do with my helpin' her with chores!"

Matt suppressed a grin. "Not a thing, Festus. Not a thing."

"I was jest trying to explain how I use my days off to do good in this town. Not that you don't, Matthew. But it don't hurt to lend a helpin' hand to them that don't happen to be your good friends."

"I couldn't agree more," Matt said, reaching for his hat. "I think it's wonderful that you are helping folks on your day off."

"You do?"

"Why sure! You're a credit to our profession and a model of unselfishness. Here I am going fishing with Doc, which is completely selfish, while you use your day off to do good for the community."

Festus puffed up a little. "I guess I am sort of proud of helpin' out on my day off instead of goin' fishin' or havin' a good time the way you do."

"And you ought to be proud, Festus. Why, Doc says that the fish are really biting down at the river and we're going to have a lot of fun. Almost makes me feel guilty after hearing what you did yesterday."

"You and Doc going to take a little hair of the dog down to the river?"

Matt shrugged. "You know that old Elmer Scroggins

pays Doc in homemade peach brandy rather than in dollars.''

"I heard that his brandy is better'n anything that Miss
Kitty can buy.''

Matt smacked his lips. "Darn right it is, Festus! And
after we catch a bunch of fish, we're going to fry and
eat 'em right on the river. Bake them over the coals
while we sip that sweet brandy and swap lies.''

"Geez, Matthew, that sure does sound like fun!''

"Maybe, but come tomorrow I won't have the satisfaction of helping people the way that you do following
your days off. Nope, I'll probably have some fish and
brandy left, but nowhere near the satisfaction that you
have right now.''

"I expect not,'' Festus said, looking mighty down for
a satisfied man. "I ain't been fishin' for an awful long
time, either.''

"Too bad,'' Matt said, grabbing his hat and heading
for the door. "But I'm sure that they'll still be bitin' the
next time you get a few minutes to drop your line.''

Matt was just about to open the door when it suddenly
swung open, nearly banging him in the face. "Marshal!
I'm glad I caught you as you were leaving.''

"What's going on?'' Matt asked Fred Paulson, the
retired minister and civic leader.

"Have you got a few minutes that we can talk in
private?''

"Well, I was . . . sure,'' Matt said, knowing that the
man would not have come over if he didn't have something pretty important on his mind.

"It's Abe,'' Paulson said before he took a seat and
Matt settled in behind his desk. "He looks terrible.''

"Doc says that he hasn't much time left,'' Matt replied. "It's a shame that such a fine man has to suffer."

"It sure is," Paulson agreed, "and only the Lord understands the why of our misery. But now Abe has even more to weigh down his poor mind, bless his soul."

"What's that?"

"Nick has been paroled from prison and is coming home."

"What!" both Matt and Festus blurted in unison.

"I'm afraid you heard me correctly," Paulson told them. "Nick has been paroled. I suppose it has something to do with the authorities wanting him to be able to pay his final respects to his father."

"Abe can't stand Nick," Festus sputtered. "Everyone in Dodge City hates Nick except maybe his mother, Flora. But nobody much likes her, either."

"I know that, but Nick is coming and poor Abe doesn't need that kind of grief during his final hours."

"You're right," Matt said, "but . . . if Nick has been paroled, I can't stop him from coming home."

"I was afraid that you'd say something like that," Paulson replied. "But what about Jessica and James?"

"What about them?"

"Well, Abe called a bunch of us together and we sort of had a little farewell party. But first, he asked us all to help watch over James and Jessica, because he's worried about what Nick will do to them when he discovers he's been completely disinherited."

"That shouldn't come as much of a surprise," Festus said. "Nick and his father have been on the outs for years."

"True, but Nick has always bragged that someday he'd inherit the Dawson Ranch because he is the eldest son."

15

"But isn't he a stepson?" Matt asked.

"That is correct. But Nick never accepted that. As far as he is concerned, he has just as legitimate a right to his father's estate as the other two. In fact, he believes that as the eldest child, he should inherit everything."

"It doesn't matter what he believes," Matt said. "Abe has the right to pass his land and holdings on to Jessica and James."

"Don't try to tell Nick that," the minister said.

Matt frowned. "I see what you are getting at and I also suspect that Flora has told Nick that Abe really was his father. She's evil enough to do something like that."

"Marshal, when the five of us left Abe's, we decided that you should know about this because we feel Abe's children are in mortal danger. And if anything happened to them, Nick would have the strongest legal claim on the ranch and everything Abe owns."

"I'm not so sure of that," Matt replied. "Especially since Abe has used you five as witnesses that he is disinheriting Nick. But I do agree that the matter bears close watching. I'll wire the prison and find out exactly when Nick is due and I'll meet him at the train station."

Paulson looked relieved. "Thank you, Matt. Just be careful. Abe is worried that Nick won't come home alone. That he'll bring other hardcases to back his claim."

"If he tries to do that, he'll be headed right back to prison," Matt said. "I might even go out and see Abe, Jessica, and James. Tell the other four of you that I'll stay on top of this."

"Bless you, Matt. You, too, Deputy Haggen. I know that you are underpaid and overworked and I'll sure support you next election."

"Thanks," Matt said.

"Matthew is goin' fishin' today, Reverend. But I'll be here if Nick arrives."

"As a matter of fact, I'm going fishing, too," Paulson said. "I hear that they are really biting right now."

"Maybe I'll see you down at the river, then," Matt said. "I was on my way over to get my fishing pole and gear right now."

"Think I'll do the same. It's way too nice a day to sit around indoors."

"You fellas have a real good time today," Festus said as they headed out. "I hope you catch a bunch of fish and, Matt, say hi to Doc!"

But Matt was already striding down the street, and so Festus was left alone to feel good about all the things he'd done yesterday on his own day off.

He was still trying to feel good a whole hour later when Mort Beeson, the owner of the Lucky Dice Saloon on the south side of the railroad tracks, came rushing into the office. "Where's Marshal Dillon!"

"He went fishin'. Why? Somethin' wrong?"

"You bet there is," Mort said, dragging out a handkerchief and mopping sweat from his brow. "There's been a bad fight. A couple of the Texans got into it over one of the girls that work at the Lucky Dice and when the dust cleared, one of them was knocked out cold and the other was so drunk he grabbed the girl and ran upstairs. He's on the roof shoutin' and carryin' on something awful! I'm afraid he's going to toss that girl off and she'll break her neck and be killed!"

Festus came out of his chair. "What's the girl's name?"

"Stella. At least, that's what she goes by. I hired her

because she's the prettiest gal south of the tracks and still young and spry. But she's a flirt and there's no doubt that she egged the two cowboys on, causing them to fight over her. That still don't mean that she ought to die for her mistake, does it?''

''Well, of course not!'' Festus checked his gun, then grabbed his floppy hat and pulled it right down to his ears so their tops bent.

''If that cowboy don't throw her off my roof and break Stella's fool neck, I'll fire her. I don't need this kind of trouble. As it is, those boys busted up my back-bar mirror and a couple of chairs and tables. I'll take it out of Stella's pay, bet on that!''

Festus didn't really care about those kinds of details. He was worried about the girl being killed and also about the cowboy maybe being so drunk and crazy that he'd throw himself off the roof with her. It would be terrible if the both of them died, and as he ran out the door, he was wondering how Matthew would handle a mess like this.

Dang it anyway, I sure wish that I was fishin'!

With Mort close behind, Festus ran across Front Street and then the railroad tracks. Sure enough, he saw a crowd of rowdy Texans out in front of the Lucky Dice staring up at a bloodied cowboy who was holding a girl far too young and pretty to be working in a low-class place like the Lucky Dice.

''What's goin' on here!'' Festus yelled, bursting through the crowd and stopping to crane his neck back and stare upward.

''Jump, you coward!'' one drunken cowboy shouted. ''Don't be afraid.''

''Throw the girl off and I'll catch her!'' another cried,

18

waving a bottle and staggering around and around. "But take her clothes off first so it'll be more fun!"

"Shut up!" Festus yelled, drawing his six-gun and firing it into the sky.

That caught their attention.

"Who are you, her father or something'?" one cowboy asked, trying not to burst out laughing. Then he looked up and shouted, "The both of you try to land on this stupid lawman!"

Festus cracked the fool across the forehead with the barrel of his gun and the cowboy's grin melted as his knees buckled and he dropped in the street. Festus glared at the others. "All of you go back inside right now, or I'll arrest the whole bunch of you and you'll get fined fifty dollars in Judge Brooker's court tomorrow!"

It was an empty threat. In the first place, Judge Brooker would only fine them ten dollars, and in the second place, the jail wouldn't hold but ten men, but the threat seemed to work. With much grumbling, the crowd slowly went back inside, leaving Festus and Mort to stand alone in the street wondering what to do next.

"What's your name?" Festus finally called up.

"Stella! Help me!"

"I know your name," Festus said. "Mort here already told me that. I'm askin' him what his name is?"

"Willy," the cowboy said, forearm wrapped around Stella like a vine and a knife clenched in his right hand. "Willy McCoy, and I love this here girl and I'm a-gonna marry and take her back home with me to Texas!"

"Willy," Festus said, "maybe you ought to sober up and rethink this a mite."

"Nope, I love Stella and she said that she loves me so that's that! And if she won't marry me, we're both gonna jump off this roof and land on our heads and at least be buried together!''

"Help me!" Stella cried again.

"What are you going to do?" Mort asked.

"I ain't exactly sure yet," Festus admitted. "I don't think he's bluffing. Did he cut up the other cowboy with that knife?"

"Yep. Didn't kill him, though. Just cut him up some. He'll be all right."

"That's good," Festus said. He looked back up. "Willy, Mort here says that you didn't cut that other cowboy up too bad. So, if you let the girl go and come on down, we can talk this thing out and then you can go back home."

"Not until she marries me!" the kid shouted.

He was a tall, skinny boy with a wild shock of red hair and freckles. He was probably handsome but one of his eyes was swollen shut and his lips were mashed. What worried Festus most, however, was that he was so drunk that he might accidentally fall off the roof, carrying the girl with him.

"Willy," Festus said, "throw down that knife."

"Why, it's mine!"

"You can have it back before you leave Dodge City. Just throw it down now."

"So you can shoot me?"

"I won't do that."

"Okay!"

Willy threw the knife right at Festus, and damned if he didn't have to move quick to keep from getting stuck! It was a big old Bowie knife and it would have killed him for certain.

"Sorry, Deputy," Willy said, not looking at all sorry.

"Now let Stella go."

"Nope. We either get married or we take a tall dive."

"Help!" the girl screamed. "I ain't ready to die!"

Festus had to admit that Stella was sure a pretty little thing. She had long golden hair and real pretty legs, what Festus could see of them, and that was more than he ought.

"I'm comin' up to talk with you, Willy! We can talk this thing out!"

Festus started into the saloon but Willy screamed, "If you go in there, I'll jump right this minute! I swear that I will!"

Stella believed him, because now she really started to screech.

"Festus, what are you going to do!" Mort demanded. "That boy means what he says."

"I know."

"Well, then?"

"I'm a-thinkin', Mort! What kind of rattlesnake juice do you pour for these cowboys!"

"Don't blame me!"

Festus took a deep breath just a-wishin' like anything that Matthew was here now instead of down by the river fishing. He considered sending Mort or someone off to find Matthew and Doc but knew that this crisis would end one way or the other before the pair could return.

"Get the preacher!" Willy shouted. "Get him right now, or so help me Gawd, we'll do a death dive!"

"Mort, Reverend Paulson was just in the office a little while ago. Go to his house and bring him on the double."

"You want him to marry them!"

"Stella!" Festus shouted. "We're in a real fix here.

21

Would you marry Willy and go back to Texas with him rather than takin' a 'death dive' into this here street?''

"Yes! I don't want to die!''

"Get Reverend Paulson!'' Festus shouted.

It seemed like forever before Paulson arrived. Up on the roof Willy kept drinking, and even Stella was taking frequent gulps from the bottle. But at least they were still alive. When the situation was explained to Paulson, he objected.

"I can't perform holy matrimony under these conditions!''

Willy heard that and shouted down, "Reverend, she said she'd marry me! Now you either marry us or you'll perform our funeral services! So which is it going to be? A wedding or a wake!''

"I don't even have my holy Bible!'' Paulson whispered.

"Fake it,'' Festus urged. "Reverend, this is no time to be stubborn! This boy is serious!''

Paulson looked up at the pair, then shook his head and dragged out what appeared to Festus to be a little prayer book, but was actually a book of hymns. Pretending to read, he threw his head back and shouted, "Do you, Willy . . . Willy what?''

"McCoy!''

"Do you, Willy McCoy, promise to love, honor, and . . . and protect this woman for the rest of your days?''

"Sure thing!''

"And do you . . . who are you?''

"Stella! Stella O'Leary!''

"Do you, Stella—''

"Wait!'' she cried. "My real name is Penelope Zyskowski.''

"Fine. Do you, Penelope, take this man to be your lawfully wedded husband. To stand with him through good and bad, rich or poor, sick, drunk, or sober?"

"Yeah, if I live long enough!"

"Then I pronounce you—"

"Wait a minute!" Willy cried. "I got to give her a wedding ring, don't I? Otherwise, it ain't legal. And I ain't got a ring!"

For a moment no one said a word, then the girl cried, "Someone give Willy a ring!"

"Oh," Mort stormed, "they can have this one I'm wearing. It's just brass and glass anyway but it looks good."

So they threw the ring up, and after fumbling around for a few minutes, Stella fitted it to her thumb.

"Okay, Preacher! Finish 'er up!" Willy crowed.

"In the name of God, I pronounce you man and wife!"

"Whooopeee!" Willy bellowed, taking a long chug on the bottle and giving the remainder of it to Stella, who emptied it a moment before Willy picked her up and swung her completely around.

Festus's heart almost stopped, because there was a moment when Willy and the girl appeared to have lost their balance and were coming off the roof. But Willy was a strong and surefooted boy and he managed to keep upright. A moment later they disappeared, and when Festus barged into the saloon, they were standing on the balcony shouting and yelling. The entire saloon burst into song and applause and Festus couldn't believe it but Willy and Stella were kissing up a storm.

"You gonna arrest him?" Mort said.

"On their wedding night? I sure ain't!"

"Dang fools is what they are," Mort swore. "And she's gonna pay for the damage."

"Why don't you ask this bunch to take up a wedding collection, then send Mr. and Mrs. McCoy over to the hotel," Festus suggested. "In the morning, we can haul 'em in and see if they want to stay married or not."

"You don't think that it was legal?"

"I asked the reverend," Festus replied, "and he told he wasn't sure if it was hisself. So I'm leavin' it up to Stella and Willy. If they're willin' to stay hitched and get out of Dodge City tomorrow, then they are the McCoys of Texas far as I'm concerned."

"You got a strange sense of serving justice," Mort Beeson growled, "but if I get my money and rid of that cowboy and Stella in one fell swoop, I'll go along with your decision."

"Glad to hear it," Festus said.

"Where is Marshal Dillon?"

"He and Doc Adams are down at the river fishin'."

"I heard they're biting like crazy. Maybe I'll take tomorrow off and go fishing myself. Want to come along, Festus?"

"Maybe," Festus said. "I could sure use some fun fer a change."

CHAPTER

3

Nick Dawson, Charlie Roe, and Moses Parker brought the rickety peddler's wagon to a standstill atop a low, windswept ridge and stared west toward the vast Dawson Ranch. All three were well dressed, thanks to a homesteader who decided that his life was easily worth $316 after they'd paid an unexpected call soon after their parole. Unfortunately, the homesteader had fallen down his well and died anyway. His livestock had brought another eighty-five dollars from a travelling peddler, who had also proved to be exceedingly generous, donating his wagon and team of horses in exchange for a merciful death and the solemn promise that he would receive a Christian burial out on the open prairie. And he would have, too, if Nick and company had taken the time and owned a decent shovel. So they'd tossed his body in the Kansas River just south of Abilene, raised a bottle in toast, and drove the wagon on through

Ellsworth then Hays, generally following the Kansas Pacific Railroad.

Nick was twenty-three, tall, dark, and considered by women to be handsome except when they looked into his cold gray eyes and saw not a shred of humanity or feeling. He wore a six-gun on his hip and he loved silver jewelry, wearing rings on five of his fingers and a silver hatband that glittered in the sunlight.

Charlie Roe would also have been considered handsome if it had not been for a savage beating he'd taken his first week in prison after refusing to hand over his dinner to a menacing giant. The whipping had been severe enough to have broken Charlie's nose, scarred his eyebrows, and knocked out his upper front teeth. But the huge and brutish convict had paid dearly a month later when Charlie had caught him alone in a supply room and used his throat to test the sharpness of his newly fashioned knife.

Moses Parker was neither handsome nor homely. He simply looked pleasant and agreeable and was the kind that attracted no notice because he was of average size with very ordinary features. What was not readily apparent about Moses was that he had once proven himself to be the finest all-around rifle and pistol shot in Kansas City. Moses still wore his July Fourth Marksman championship belt buckle as a reminder of his surprising victory over much older and more seasoned shootists. But that was almost ten years ago and a man could not live on his reputation alone, so Moses had become a buffalo hunter, then when the buffalo were all shot out, a wolfer, and finally a bounty hunter. He had loved each and every killing occupation, but especially bounty hunting. Unfortunately, a woman of some influence had seen him ambush a chicken thief in one of Omaha's back alleys and convinced the townspeople that Moses's action was far too severe for the offense. Unflappable as ever, Moses had pleaded guilty but argued that if horse thieves were fair game and candidates for hanging, why not a chicken thief, the only difference being that chickens were far tastier and better egg providers. His boyish smile and unwavering good humor had won over a jury and earned him a ridiculously short prison sentence.

Now, however, they were nearing Dodge City and the place where the real action was about to begin. Nick had explained everything, but had been careful not to dwell on Marshal Dillon or Deputy Festus Haggen.

"This is fine ranching country," Charlie allowed, the clean cool wind whistling through where his teeth had once resided. "How many acres do you stand to inherit?"

"Just shy of twenty-four thousand," Nick replied. "And I have no idea how many cattle, sheep, and horses."

"Your pa owns sheep?" Moses asked with surprise.

"That's right. He owns whatever makes money and he has both Mexican and Indian shepherds that go into the mountains in the summer and feed off on his north range during the winter. But when I take over, I'll fire 'em and sell off the woollies. I hate 'em."

Nick started thinking about how Abe had driven him and his poor mother off this ranch when he wasn't but thirteen or fourteen. It had been hard on his ma, but she'd showed Abe and everyone else what she was made of and had made a good living running her saloon.

"That ranch should belong to me," he declared, standing with his boots planted wide apart beside the peddler's wagon. "I am the eldest son, maybe not by blood, but by legal adoption. And by Gawd, justice will be done."

"It sure is some spread," Moses said. "But I'll bet your pa has got a lot of men on his payroll. This won't be easy."

"Nothing is easy," Nick said. "But this is better than anything you ever dreamed about. It's just going to take a little time and some planning. We can't just ride in there and expect to take the ranch over. We got to be smart and we got to be patient."

"So how are we going to do it?" Moses asked.

"We'll wait until an hour or so before sundown," Nick said, putting his plan into words and thinking as he talked. "I'll hide in the wagon. You and Charlie can ride up front and pose as peddlers."

"Not a good idea," Moses said, frowning.

"Why not?"

"Well, in the first place, Charlie looks butt ugly and mean as hell with his front teeth missing and all those scars."

"Now wait a doggone minute!" Charlie growled. "I—"

Moses raised his hand and smiled. "I didn't mean to insult you, Charlie, and I was about to say that the real problem is that I never seen two peddlers sellin' outta the same wagon. Have you?"

"No, I guess not," Charlie admitted. "But what am I supposed to do?"

"You can hide in back with me," Nick decided. "They'll want to see what Moses has to sell, but you think of some excuse to hold 'em off until morning. Later, when everyone in the bunkhouse is asleep, you and me can go into the house and have a serious talk with Abe."

"You gonna kill him?" Charlie asked.

"I don't know," Nick replied. "But I sure ain't going to leave without him giving me title to the ranch."

"But you said he'd never do that. And if he's already dying, what can we do to make him change his mind?"

"I think I know what will change his mind," Nick said quietly.

"What?"

"Jessica and James." Nick spat out their names like vile curses. "The old man loves them two more than his own life."

Charlie smiled. "I get it, we force the old man to write up a new will giving everything to you, then we kill your brother and sister anyway!"

"I don't know about the last part," Nick hedged. "We can't do that without bringing the law down on our heads. But if we don't do anything stupid, we can win it all."

"How you gonna get away with killin' the old man after he changes his will?" Moses asked.

Nick shrugged. "I hear he's already on death's doorstep. It shouldn't be too hard to push him over the edge and make it look natural."

"What about me and the crew?" Moses asked. "When they wake up in the morning and find you and Charlie in the big house and with the old man dead—"

"They won't," Nick said, suddenly seeing the way it should be done. "We'll get Abe to change his will so that I inherit everything, then kill him and light out for Dodge City in the dark. Moses, in the morning, you play it dumb. We still got a few goods in the wagon. Not much, but enough to make you look legitimate. Then you leave and come into Dodge. But don't let on you know me and Charlie."

"Then you take the new will to a lawyer and we take over the ranch!" Moses said, slapping his side. "What a great plan! Nick, you're sure a hell of a lot smarter than you look!"

Nick managed a smile, but it quickly turned hard when he said, "Just don't ever try to cross me up, either of you, or I'll outsmart you, too."

"Hey!" Charlie protested. "We're all going to be rich! Why the hell would we try and double-cross our meal ticket?"

"He's right." Moses bristled. "And I don't much like to be threatened."

"No threat," Nick told them both. "Just a promise that . . . if you ever decide to try and deal me a hand from the bottom of the deck . . . I'll find a way to get even."

After that warning, Nick walked away and rolled a cigarette. He knew that he'd angered his partners, but now that he stood before what he would have for his own, he figured that he ought to start distancing himself from Moses and Charlie. After all, he'd be the boss and they'd work for him. This meant that like it or not, they were just going to have to start showing him a little more respect.

Nick and Charlie hid under a blanket and Moses drove. Nick was glad that his partners didn't realize how worried he was as they entered the ranch because Abe had sworn to have him horsewhipped if he ever returned. And that ornery old weasel would do it, too! Nick thought about how fine it would be to fire Hannibal. The

Dawson Ranch foreman had gotten so he thought he was something real special, and taking the old man down was long overdue.

It took nearly an hour before the ranch came into view and the sun was just a fading fireball on the western horizon when Moses drew up before the cookshack and called, "Hey, anybody home!"

Hannibal was the first one out the door. "What are you doin' here, mister?"

"Well," Moses replied, "I was hoping to sell you and your men a few goods and maybe put up for the night, if it ain't askin' too much."

"What do you have for sale?" the foreman asked.

"Just some odds and ends."

"We'll put you up for the night in the bunkhouse but we don't like peddlers coming onto the ranch, so you'll be leaving first thing in the morning."

"Fair enough," Moses said. "I sure am hungry and I can smell food cookin'."

"There's plenty. I'll have one of the boys drive your wagon over to the barn and unhitch your team."

Nick froze, then relaxed when Moses said, "These horses are kind of ornery and I'd as soon unhitch 'em myself. Don't want to be a bother or have someone pawed, kicked, or bit. That would most likely anger you."

"It would for a fact," Hannibal said. "All right, then, put your team in that empty corral yonder and then come on over and have something to eat. We rise before dawn and get an early start."

"How far is it to Dodge City?" Moses asked.

"Twelve miles south."

"Then I'll be there by noon," Moses said, driving the

wagon off. When they were alone, he looked inside and whispered, "Nick, how am I doin'?"

"Just fine. You've done your part and now we do ours."

Moses nodded. "You'd better make real sure you don't raise a ruckus in the big house or these boys will come swarmin' in like hornets. If that happens, they'll figure out that you were smuggled in on this wagon and I'll be in a mess of trouble."

"We'll see you in Dodge City," Nick said, slipping out of the back of the wagon behind Charlie. "But remember, you don't know us."

"Mind tellin' me why?"

"Moses, how many lawmen have you killed in your day?"

"Just one."

"Well, you might get to kill a couple more in the next few weeks."

Moses began to unhitch the horses as he chuckled. "Well, Nick, you know that shootin' things is what I do best."

When the horses were turned into the empty corral, Moses grabbed his saddlebag and headed for the cookshack to eat and then to join the cowboys and palaver awhile before turning in early. Nick and Charlie waited in the barn until the hour grew late and all the lights went off.

"Man oh man." Charlie sighed. "I'm sure hungry. Do you think that there's plenty of food in the big house kitchen and maybe some whiskey?"

"No whiskey," Nick said. "We'll have a long walk tonight and we can't afford to make any mistakes, or we're dead men. But we can celebrate when we reach Dodge City in the morning.''

"Twelve miles," Charlie said. "I sure wish that I was Moses bunkin' down tonight after a good feed.''

"But then you'd miss seeing my father die.''

"I forgot about that," Charlie admitted. "How much longer do we have to wait?''

"Not long," Nick replied. "I want to give James and Jessica time to fall asleep. The old man has a Mexican couple that cook and do housekeeping, but they're harmless as flies.''

"I'm looking forward to seeing his face when he sees yours," Charlie said. "And I was thinking some about how we could make it look like he died accidentally.''

"Yeah?''

"Yeah. Want to hear some of my ideas?''

"Sure," Nick said, deciding that he would wait just a little longer before they finally paid old man Dawson his last visit.

It was well past midnight when Nick and Charlie slipped into the big two-story ranch house and then crept upstairs and down the dark hallway to Abe Dawson's bedroom. When they opened the door, they could hear Abe's labored snoring. Moonlight filtered through the windows, allowing Nick to see well enough to tiptoe over and light a small lamp on the bedside table. Abe did not awaken.

"Holy cow," Charlie whispered, staring. "I expected a lot more man than that.''

"He used to be quite a man," Nick said, studying a lined and sickness-ravaged face that he barely recognized. "In fact, he used to be a hell of a big man.''

"Well, he sure ain't no more," Charlie said. "I'll bet he don't weigh much more'n a hundred pounds."

Nick figured that would be about right. Abraham Dawson was all bones and slack flesh. You could see the lines of deep suffering left by his disease. He shook his head and muttered, "If I ever got that sick, I'd at least have the guts to shoot myself."

"Me, too. Wake him up."

Nick removed his Barlow pocketknife, unfolded the long blade, and placed it lightly against Abe's throat. The old man stirred and Nick actually had to cut him a little before his eyes opened. When they did, though, they went as big and round as saucers.

"Nick?" The old man tried to sit up but Nick easily pushed him back down. Suddenly he was very much enjoying himself.

"Yes, Father, in the flesh."

"What are you doing here!"

"I come to say a last farewell," Nick said. "Along with my friend Charlie."

"Get out!"

Nick placed the cupped palm of his hand over Abe's mouth, causing the old man to struggle and then attempt to tear it away. But Abe had no strength left and failed.

"I'm going to ask Charlie to go over to your desk and bring us some paper and ink. Then you're going to write a new will. A very short one making me the sole inheritor of the ranch."

Abe's muffled protest did not go unnoticed by Charlie, who said, "I don't think he wants to help you out, Nick."

Nick leaned harder, crushing Abe's lips. It was, he thought, hard to believe that this was the man he had once so admired and then later feared and hated. "Father," he said sarcastically, "I am hurt that you would want to disinherit me! I'll bet you intended to leave everything to Jessica and James, didn't you?"

Abe managed to nod his head.

"Well," Nick said, "that's too bad. Because right after Charlie brings me the paper and ink, I'm going to send him down to pay a little visit to Jessica. He's going to slit her throat. How would you like that?"

Abe's renewed struggles showed that he didn't like it at all.

"And Father," Nick said, leaning close, "after Jessica, Charlie is to come back here and see how the writing goes. If you're still of a mind not to help us, then I'm going to send him back down the hallway to pay a visit to James. I expect that James will also die drowning in his own blood."

Abe stopped struggling and Nick grinned. "Father, don't tell me. Have you just decided to cooperate?"

Abe nodded.

"Charlie, find the paper and ink. Father has had a big change of heart."

They forced him to use the last shreds of his strength to write a simple will and date it just moments before Charlie spotted an apple core over on the desk. It wasn't fresh and he had some difficulty prying Abe's mouth open and shoving it down his throat until it was lodged in his windpipe.

"I'm just trying to help make you healthy. Remember how an 'apple a day keeps the doctor away'? Well, old man"—Charlie giggled—"you sure ain't going to need no more doctorin'!"

Abraham Dawson died choking and thrashing. It was a show, Nick thought, well worth waiting for.

CHAPTER

4

Matt joined Kitty at the Delmonico Restaurant for breakfast that morning while Festus made the usual rounds. Their table was always the one reserved by the front window so Matt could keep an eye on the street, just in case his presence was suddenly required. It was a fine day in early September and most of the cattle that had been driven up from Texas had been sold and shipped out already. There were a few buyers still hanging around Dodge City, but most of them had departed along with the cowboys.

"I'll miss the excitement," Kitty was saying. "When the Texans go back home, it suddenly feels pretty dead around here."

"There are an awful lot of people in town who would disagree with you." Matt sipped his coffee, then added, "Starting with Festus and me."

"Oh, come on now," Kitty argued. "I remember last

winter when we had that weeklong snowstorm. You said that you sure were anxious for spring and the drovers to arrive.''

"I said that?"

"Yep. Plenty of times, in fact. You may not admit it, and you may get pretty weary of all the trouble, but you don't like it peaceful too long. You get restless, even irritable.''

Matt grunted. "Maybe that's so, but Festus and I don't get much rest while the cowboys are in town with cash to spend. You're on the sane side of the tracks and you forget what it's like on the other side."

"I haven't forgotten," Kitty replied. "Every time I hear the gunshots at night I worry that you or Festus or even Doc are walking into an ambush."

"Festus and I are real careful. Most of the trouble is just some cowboy or two getting a snoot full of liquor and misbehaving. You have girls and you know what kinds of trouble they can create among homesick cowboys and lovesick fools."

"Oh yes," Kitty said with a smile. "I can't hardly hire a pretty girl because they up and get married inside of a month. And the ugly ones don't bring in the business. I like the sort of middle-of-the-road kinds of girls who attract men but do not make them crazy. When I get a girl like that, there's a good chance that she'll stick with me a year or two."

"That may be true," Matt said, "but you're a natural-born matchmaker. How many of your girls have you married off?"

"Seventeen and counting," Kitty said with a smile. "Trouble is, I can't get myself married off."

"You could if you wanted."

She looked him right in the eye. "I just haven't had the right man ask me . . . yet."

Matt could feel his cheeks warming. "Kitty, I—"

"That's all right," she interrupted. "I'm a successful and very patient woman. I'm having a real good time. Best time by far of my life, so don't go feeling sorry for me, Marshal Dillon."

"I'd never do that," he told her. "You're strong-willed and independent. I'm not sure that you could put up with a husband."

"I could with the right one. Maybe someday, huh?"

"Maybe," he said, taking a sudden interest in his cup of coffee. Matt knew Kitty's history just as well as he knew his own, because they'd been friends . . . and more, for a long, long time. Kitty had lost her mother at an early age and her father, John Russell, was a trav-elling gambler who'd never given her the time of day. Fortunately, Kitty had been adopted and raised by a wonderful couple who had protected but never suffo-cated her. Kitty had her own wild and restless streak and Matt always wondered if she really was marrying ma-terial. The woman loved to travel and would often leave the Long Branch in her faithful bartender and manager's hands and go away for weeks at a time. Kitty never really talked about where she went and Matt had even wondered if she had another lover, perhaps one in Kan-sas City or St. Louis. But he knew better than to ask.

"Would you look at that rattletrap peddler's wagon," Kitty said. "I wonder what he has for sale other than hard times."

Matt turned to the street. The wagon in question was indeed a sorry-looking affair, but its driver was smiling and waving to everyone as if he were running for town mayor. "I've never seen that one before."

"Me neither. By the looks of his horses, though, he hasn't got much of value."

"I expect that you will find that out soon enough," Matt replied. "You or one of your girls."

"Oh sure. All of us miss having some variety in the places we shop. The selection here in Dodge is not the best. If a local merchant gets a new dress or bonnet in, you can bet it won't last long. And often, they buy them in identical lots so that when you do get the first one you quickly realize that half the other women in town are wearing the same outfit. It's awful, Matt."

"I can see that," Matt said, knowing that Kitty did almost all of her shopping out of town and had a wardrobe that was the envy of every woman in Dodge City. "Uh-oh, here comes Festus."

"And it looks like big trouble," Kitty decided. "Festus doesn't break into a run unless it's pretty serious."

Matt reached into his pocket for money but Kitty covered his hand. "I'm buying this morning."

"You paid yesterday and the day before," Matt protested. "Kitty, you buy me a lot more meals than I buy you."

"That's because I make a lot more money."

"But—"

"It's all right, Matt. Just see what's bothering Festus. I'll take care of the bill."

He was always uncomfortable about letting Kitty pay. But they enjoyed each other so much that he couldn't figure out how to solve the problem and Kitty did make many times his salary. In fact, Matt suspected she was a wealthy woman.

He came to his feet, eyes on Festus, who looked real upset. And when Festus got upset, he had a tendency to tell everyone exactly what was wrong. Matt did not want their business to become common knowledge, so he was eager to intercept his deputy before he could reach the restaurant and blurt out whatever was bothering him. "Kitty, I'll see you later. Thanks again."

"Anytime," she replied, looking worried as he hurried out the door.

"Matthew, we got big troubles!" Festus hollered.

"Simmer down and hold it until we get to the office," Matt said, taking his deputy's arm and guiding him up the street.

"You won't believe who I saw at the Red Dog Saloon!"

Matt had a pretty good idea. "Nick Dawson."

Festus stopped dead in this tracks. "Well, how did you guess that!"

"Because what other saloon except his mother's would Nick go to? Flora will give him free food and drinks and try to protect him. Why would he go anyplace else?"

"Yeah," Festus said, shaking his head. "Why would he?"

They went into the marshal's office and Matt poured Festus a cup of coffee, then decided to have another himself, although he usually quit at four cups before noon. "All right, why don't you tell me exactly what happened."

"Well, sir, I was a-makin' my rounds as usual. I waltzed down Front Street, then up First Avenue. Checked out Walnut and Chestnut streets and talked awhile with some good old boys at the Odd Fellows

Hall. They're havin' a pancake breakfast to raise some money for Elmer Hopkins. You know that Elmer has fallen on hard times and—''

"Festus, get to where you first saw Nick Dawson."

"Oh, yeah. Well, after I left them boys at the Odd Fellows, I moseyed up Bridge Street. Saw Bud Flowers sitting on the porch at the Wright House Hotel. He's not feelin' too sprightly either. Then I found Louie Pheeters drunk as a loon sleepin' behind the—''

"Festus!"

"Sorry, Matthew. You know I have a tendency to ramble a bit. But I was walkin' past Ham Bell's Livery when, right out of the corner of my eye, I saw Nick Dawson. He was headin' into his ma's saloon with another fella."

Matt leaned forward slightly, coffee forgotten. "What did the other fella look like?"

"I couldn't see his face but he was kind of tall and slim, like Nick. Anyway, I follered them into that there saloon and walked right up to Nick and I said, 'What are you a-doin' in Dodge City?' ''

"I would have been better if you'd have just come and gotten me," Matt advised.

"I didn't want to interrupt your breakfast with Miss Kitty. And besides, I recollect you sayin' that there was nothing you could do to arrest Nick if he was let out of prison."

"That's right. So what happened then?"

"Well, sir, Nick offered to buy me a whiskey! He said that I looked like I needed a drink . . . which I kinda did at that moment. I told him that I was on duty and couldn't drink, so he said he'd drink one extra for me."

"What about the other man?"

"Well, now, he sort of moseyed over into a corner and was talkin' to old Flora. His back was to me, so I still couldn't see him too well. But Flora, she came stompin' over and she gave me hell. Said that I wasn't welcome in the Red Dog and neither were you. And I told her we could dang sure go wherever we wanted to in this town any old time we wanted."

"And she said?"

"Flora said that wasn't true. That we couldn't just barge into people's bedrooms and the like any old time. I told her that we never did that anyway and Nick, dog-gone his hide, he got to laughin'."

"He thought it was funny?"

"Yep! Then everyone in Flora's saloon got to laughin' like a bunch of hyenas and so I just turned and left. I came lookin' to see what you wanted me to do next."

"You did just right," Matt told him.

"I did?"

"Yes." Matt frowned. "I can't arrest Nick, but thanks to you, we can sure keep an eye on him."

"But what about Abraham Dawson? He told them old friends of his that Nick might even try to kill James and Jessica."

"That's why I'd better get out to his ranch this morning and warn them that Nick has arrived. I also want to have a good look at Nick's friend. Could be he's a wanted man and we can haul him into jail and get some information."

"Well, Matthew, that's a real good idea! But since I couldn't see his face—"

"Don't worry about it," Matt said. "We'll have plenty of chances to see him before long. You can bet that they'll cross over to this side of the tracks. Kitty likes to hire plain girls but they are still the prettiest in town, and Nick has always considered himself quite the ladies' man. He'll probably show up at the Long Branch a lot sooner than Kitty would like.''

"I better warn her, too," Festus said. "You ridin' out now?"

"I am," Matt told him. "From what I've heard, Abe Dawson might even have passed away already. He was on death's door when he called his friends in a while ago."

"Maybe that's for the best," Festus said.

"Why?"

"Because it'd just worry him so about James and Jessica. And him being so sick, he couldn't do a thing to help them."

"I hadn't thought of it like that," Matt said, "but you're probably right. Abe was such a strong man that he must have found it hard to be sick and helpless. It'd be a mercy for him to pass on. Hannibal will hold things together for the next few years until James is ready to take control."

"Hannibal is a good man," Festus agreed. "And he loves Abe's kids like they was his own."

"I know that," Matt said. "I'll be back this afternoon. Hold the lid on things."

"What if Nick starts trouble?"

"He won't," Matt predicted. "He's just out of prison and the last thing he wants to do is land in our jail. Besides, Flora will keep him under control for a while. She's the only one that he ever listened to and he needs her for protection."

"Protection from what?" Festus asked, looking confused.

"From me," Matt said, eyes tightening at the corners. "The last time I arrested Nick, I warned him that everything from our jail to Judge Brooker would be a whole lot harder."

"Well, he sure didn't look too worried when I just saw him," Festus fretted.

"That's because he isn't as smart as he thinks he is," Matt said, going out the door.

He had not ridden five miles north before he was met by James and two of Dawson's cowboys. James was red-eyed and the cowboys were grim-faced. "Marshal," James said, "if you're coming to pay last respects to my father, I'm afraid that you are too late. He passed away last night."

"I'm sorry to hear that. I expect that he died peacefully."

"I don't know. He looked like he just couldn't breathe anymore."

"Why are you going to town?"

"To get the undertaker, Mr. Crump."

"He'll do a fine job," Matt told the young rancher. Then he looked to the cowboys, whose names he could not remember. "Keep a close eye on James because Nick showed up this morning."

James paled. "This morning?"

"That's right. Festus saw him at his mother's Red Dog Saloon."

James's jaw muscles corded. "He'd better not try to set foot on the ranch or come to the funeral."

"I expect he will," Matt said.

"If he does," one of cowboys added, "Hannibal will shoot him on sight."

"That would be a bad mistake," Matt said, feeling their explosive anger. "And I'm going to order the three of you to stay on this side of the tracks. I don't want you anywhere near the Red Dog, especially while I'm at your ranch seeing what I can do to help. Is that understood?"

James stuck out his jaw the way he did when he got stubborn.

"I mean it!" Matt ordered, putting authority in his voice. "You men have no business bracing Nick. He's been released from prison and he has a right to be in town. I don't need to have trouble with you boys in addition to everything else. Am I making myself clear? Because if not, then you can turn your horses around this minute and we'll all ride together to the ranch."

"We'll stay away from him," James promised. "If there is to be trouble, it will come later, out of respect for my father."

"Any 'trouble' we have with Nick is *my* concern and will be handled by me and Deputy Haggen. So go to town, take care of business, and ride on back. I don't want to see you when I return to Dodge."

Matt left them then and continued north. He knew that they were glaring resentfully at his back and were mad as hell but he did not really care.

When he rode into the ranch yard, there were cowboys standing around looking as though they'd lost their best friend. And in a way, they had. Abraham Dawson had been a tough but fair employer and a man that never asked anyone to do a job that he would not and could not do even better himself. He had been a bronc buster and a fine roper as well as a shrewd businessman and investor. Most of all, he had been a man of honor, whose handshake was better than any contract ever devised by a lawyer.

"Matt," Hannibal said, coming over to greet him. "I expect that you met James, Roddy, and Tom heading out to get the undertaker."

"I did. I'm real sorry. How is Miss Dawson holding up?"

"As well as you could expect."

Hannibal removed his hat and ran his thick fingers through a shock of silver hair. He was probably only in his forties but this tough outdoor ranching life aged a man and Abe's death hadn't helped either. Matt knew that they'd been more like brothers than owner and foreman.

"I guess I'll pay my respects to Miss Dawson," Matt said. "And I want to talk to her in private."

"Trouble?"

"I'm afraid so," Matt said. "And I sure appreciate that this is not the best time for it to happen, but you better know that Nick showed up in town this morning."

Hannibal's eyes turned as hard as agate. "If he tries to come here, I'll have him shot dead."

"No, you won't," Matt replied. "Because then I'd have to arrest you for murder and you wouldn't be able to help James run this ranch until he's ready to do it on his own. And you wouldn't be able to protect Jessica from troubles."

The anger went out of Hannibal almost as fast as it had come and his broad shoulders slumped. "You're right, Matt. But I could have someone else kill him."

"Don't even think about it," Matt warned.

"Why not? You know that he'll want part of Mr. Dawson's estate and do anything necessary to get something from James and Jessica."

"What Nick wants and what he can get are two far different matters. I assume that Abraham wrote a formal will."

"Sure. Judge Blasdell helped him write it and it's in his possession. The old judge wouldn't allow Mr. Dawson to go to anyone else."

"Then I don't see how there could be any legal basis for Nick to lay claim to a single dollar, much less the land and cattle."

"Yeah, I guess you're right. And there's also the witnesses that Mr. Dawson called in. You know, he trusted in his friends and he wanted them to know his wishes in person. To hear them from his own lips. It wasn't easy, but he did it anyway."

"Mr. Dawson never took the easy way out of anything," Matt said, placing his hand on the foreman's slumped shoulders. "I'm sorry. I know how much you'll miss him."

"Yeah," Hannibal said, "it sure won't be the same. But James is a good kid and he's going to do just fine. Jessica, too."

"Do you know what her plans are?"

"No. I figured we'd wait awhile to talk. Mr. Dawson wanted her to go off to an Eastern finishing school and maybe, now that he's gone, she will. I personally think it would be best if she got away."

"Perhaps so," Matt said as he passed on toward the house. It was a big, Colonial-looking two-story with an impressive veranda. The front room was cavernous and Matt had been inside enough to know his way around.

"Señor Matthew," Manuel Diaz said, coming forward to meet him. "This is a very sad time for us all. Can I get you some food or drink?"

"No," Matt said to the houseman. "I just came to offer my condolences. Is Jessica up to seeing me?"

"I will ask her."

"I'd also like to pay a moment of respect to Abe. Is his body upstairs?"

"*Sí*. You go now. I will speak to the señorita."

Matt climbed the staircase and went into Abe's room. He had seen the old cattleman about a month previously and had been shocked by his appearance but he wasn't prepared for the look on Abe's face. The old man's face was purplish and his eyes were wide open and staring. Pennies lay at the sides of his cheeks and Matt was sure that Manuel had tried to close the eyes but they would not stay shut.

It took a moment for Matt to gather his composure and then he walked over to the bedside and studied Abraham's ghostly-looking face. Matt was no doctor but he'd seen more than his share of dead men and a few that had been murdered by strangulation. That's what it looked like had happened to Abe.

Matt examined the corpse's neck for finger marks and found none. Then he did something that he shouldn't have . . . he pried open the man's mouth and that's when he saw the tip of the apple core. It was unmistakable, because the stem of the apple was protruding over the man's swollen tongue, like a worm coming up out of Abe's throat. Matt closed the mouth and then turned and hurriedly left the bedroom.

His meeting with Jessica was brief. She looked terrible and Matt doubted that she heard even half of his words of condolence. Fortunately, she was young and resilient. She'd regain her normal good spirits before long and he sincerely hoped that she would decide to go back east to a finishing school. Otherwise, she might grieve too long.

"I'll do whatever I can to help with the funeral arrangements and we'll get Doc Adams to see your father."

"Why?"

Matt realized his mistake too late. The last thing that he wanted to do was to tell this girl that her father had died of suffocation and that, at least to Matt's way of thinking, it looked rather suspicious the way the apple was stuffed so deep into Abe's gullet.

"Why?"

"I . . . I meant that Doc would want to pay his personal respects before the funeral. You know that he and your father were very close."

"Of course," she said, eyes turning dull and distant again.

Matt excused himself and headed outside. He could hear crying in the kitchen and he just wanted to get away. This was no time to tell them all that Nick had returned. That bit of awful news could wait a little while longer.

CHAPTER

5

On the way back to town, Matt met the cowboys and Percy Crump heading back to the ranch house. Percy was driving his hearse wagon and dressed all in black with his mortician's silk top hat. It was a very somber procession and there wasn't much conversation when they passed each other.

"Marshal," Crump said, "these are sad circumstances."

"They are," Matt agreed. "When is the funeral?"

"Tomorrow. I forgot, but would you please ask Reverend Paulson to conduct the services."

James looked at the mortician. "What is the best time?"

"Five o'clock in the afternoon would be proper and give folks time to close their shops and attend."

"All right, then," James said, riding on.

"I'll tell the reverend," Matt called after them and the hearse wagon.

When he returned to Dodge, the first thing Matt did was go to visit Doc. "You got a minute?" he asked.

"For you, always. What can I do for you, Matt? You look awful grim."

"I rode out to the Dawson Ranch and paid my last respects to old Abraham, James, and Jessica."

"I saw James and a couple of his cowboys wearing the same expression you have on your face right now. That's when I learned about old Abe dying. It's a blessing, because our friend was in a lot of pain. Even laudanum didn't seem to help much."

"Doc, I'd like you to examine the body."

"Why? I've been treating that poor man weekly and I don't need anyone to tell me why he died."

"What if I told you Abe looked to me like he'd been strangled?"

Doc used his forefinger to scrub the pencil mustache under his nose the way he often did when confronted by a vexing question. "Then I'd say that Abe might indeed have been strangled. His lungs were filling with fluids and I expect that he drowned. But who out there would have done him in?"

"Only one person comes to my mind."

"Matt, I'm in no mood for guessing games and I've got a room full of sick patients waiting, so just spit it out."

"Nick might have killed him. Who else would have so much to gain?"

Doc shook his head. "It doesn't make any sense. In the first place, how could he have gotten into Abraham's bedroom without being seen, much less on the ranch?"

"I don't know, but he's exceptionally clever."

"I believe your imagination is running wild on you. Did you think to examine Abe's neck for bruises?"

"I did and found none, but he could have been suffocated with a pillow, couldn't he?"

"Sure, but—"

"Doc," Matt interrupted, removing his hat and running his hands through his hair. "I know I shouldn't have done it, but I opened Abe's mouth and I swear that there is a piece of apple jammed down his throat."

"Maybe he was hungry just before he died and accidentally choked on it. It happens all the time to healthy people. Abe was ill, and only semiconscious at the last."

"You are probably right but I'd still like your medical opinion."

Doc sighed. "Percy Crump won't be pleased. You know how much he resents anyone messing with his latest 'client.'"

"I don't care. Do it as a favor and then let me know what you think."

"I will," Doc promised. "How is Miss Dawson holding up?"

"Pretty well. Hannibal looks considerably worse."

"I knew that he'd take Abe's death real hard." Doc peeked around the corner and out to his waiting room. "Well, I've got some clients of my own to take care of. I'll stop by the undertaker's office first thing tomorrow morning."

"I'd rather you did it when the hearse wagon arrives."

"You're sure pushy today, Matt. What's the burr on for?"

"You didn't see Abe's face, Doc."

"We've both seen our share of dead faces and they're never pretty."

"I saw fear in Abe's eyes. No, I saw more than that," Matt continued. "I saw terror."

"What?"

"I know it sounds crazy, but we both knew Abe and the man wasn't afraid of anything. You know he had made his peace and was ready to die."

"Yeah, but—"

"That's not the look I saw in his eyes, Doc. Or on his face."

Doc patted the marshal on the shoulder. "I'll pay the undertaker a visit as soon as he arrives," he promised. "And then I'll come over to your office and let you know what I think."

"Much obliged. And I guess that you heard Nick is over at the Red Dog Saloon."

"Sure. Everyone in town is talking about it. Nick has always attracted more than his share of attention."

Matt started to leave. "Doc," he said, pausing in the doorway, "call it a gut feeling or a lawman's instincts, but the timing between Nick's arrival and Abraham's death makes me real suspicious."

"I can understand why it would, but there is no way that Nick could have gotten to Abe without someone seeing him either coming or going. There are too many people living and working on the Dawson Ranch."

"You got me there," Matt admitted just before leaving.

When he returned to his office, Festus had Louie Pheeters locked up in the jail cell. Louie was snoring away on the cell bunk. Matt glanced at him and said, "What'd he do this time?"

"He was peein' on the front window of the Lone Star Saloon and yellin' his head off because he said they wouldn't pay him for cleanin' their spittoons early this morning."

"If they didn't pay him, how'd he get enough money to get drunk?"

"Well," Festus answered, "he cleans most of the spittoons in Dodge City. Louie tells me he's got a regular business goin' and it's a pretty good one at that."

"I'll bet," Matt said. "Well, paid or not, he can't be relieving himself in public. Did you have a stern talk with Louie?"

"Oh, I tried," Festus said, "but he was too drunk to listen. I'll talk to him again when he's sober."

"You tell him that if we haul him before Judge Brooker, he's going to stay in jail a good long while. And you know what that means."

"It means he wouldn't be able to have a drink," Festus answered. "Matthew, you know that he sort of goes crazy when he can't have a drop regularly. It might even kill him to go a full week."

"Kill him or cure him," Matt said, his mind really on Abraham Dawson and that apple stem peeking out of his throat. It was a haunting memory and one he wished he'd never seen. "Anything going on in town while I was gone?"

"No, sir! Quiet as a church collection."

"And you didn't go over to the Red Dog."

"Nope. You told me not to, so I didn't."

Matt was tired and hungry. "I'm going to get a bite to eat and then I'll pay Flora and Nick a visit."

"I'd better come along."

"You've been on duty all day."

"So have you, only my day was easier," Festus argued. "I think I ought to come with you."

"All right," Matt agreed. "Let's both go eat and then pay Flora Dawson a visit."

On the way over to a nearby restaurant that Festus favored because of its stew, they had the misfortune to bump into Nathan Burke. Nathan was the town gossip and a freight agent.

"Marshal Dillon, what, exactly, are you going to do about Nick Dawson showing up on the same day his poor father dies?"

"What do you mean?"

"I mean, everyone knows that he's going to cause trouble. I can't believe that he was actually paroled so soon."

"We were a bit surprised ourselves," Matt said. "But I telegraphed the prison and they confirmed it."

"Well, then arrest the man before he commits another terrible outrage on one of our citizens!"

"I can't arrest him for no good reason," Matt said. "He may be a bad apple but he's still a citizen of these United States of America with all its rights provided by the Constitution."

"Constitution, my behind! You know that man is here to seek revenge on you and probably a lot of other people. And I'm sure that Judge Brooker would—"

"He'd say the same thing that I just told you," Matt snapped. "No crime, no arrest. Now, was there something else you wanted to say? If not, Festus and I are hungry."

Burke wasn't pleased. "You know, Marshal, vigilantism wasn't such a bad idea on this frontier."

Matt had started to pass, but now he stopped and

turned around. He knew that Burke was a rabble-rouser and could be a troublemaker, though he was well intentioned. "Nathan, don't you ever let me hear you mention that word again. Is that understood?"

Burke colored with anger. "Well," he huffed, "seems to me that I might be remembering this conversation the next time there is an election."

"Fine," Festus told him. "Now git on home to your wife and kids and stop blowin' so much hot air!"

The man stomped away and Matt shook his head. "Festus, there are times when working for the public is by far the hardest part of our jobs."

"You got that right, Matthew."

They didn't talk much over their stew. Matt was thinking about Nick Dawson and his mother and how they would react when he and Festus entered the Red Dog, and he was pretty sure that Festus was thinking along the same lines.

"I guess you know about Nick being back in town," the owner of the restaurant said as they paid their bill. "I sure don't envy you trying to arrest him again."

"It'll work out," Matt said.

"How was the stew?"

"Good as ever," Festus said, wiping a generous gob of gravy off his shirtfront with the back of his sleeve. "Wish you'd had some apple pie tonight, though. I was sorta countin' on some of it."

"Maybe tomorrow night," the man said. "You men going over to arrest Nick right now?"

"No," Matt said. "But we are going to pay him a little visit and let him know that he's being watched by everyone in the town."

"You ain't going to arrest him?"

"Can't," Festus said. "Not until he commits a crime."

"Hellfire, Marshal! He's going to kill someone sooner or later. Why wait?"

Festus started to explain the way Matt had, but changed his mind when Matt started out the door.

The Red Dog was busy and filled with the usual collection of down-and-outers. Flora Dawson served the cheapest liquor in town and liked to brag that it was strong enough to dissolve a horseshoe in less than a week. Matt had never actually seen this happen, but there were some who had and swore that Flora was telling the truth. If so, it was the only thing she ever told the truth about. It was said that she was once a dancer like Lola Montez and that she invented the original Spider Dance, where cloth spiders were sewn into the hem of her dress and made to dance as if they dangled on webs. Flora was still tall but she'd gone to pot from hard living. She smoked a corncob pipe or a cigarette, depending which one was closest at hand, and she drank her own liquor. Her face was lined and blotched with liver spots and she had the sharpest and saltiest tongue of any saloon owner on this side of the tracks. She liked to hire big, fat women to service her clients; most of them could whip the men they satisfied.

The moment that Matt walked inside he smelled the stench of vomit and urine. The floor was covered with dirty sawdust and the lamps were smoky because Flora filled them with the cheapest grade of kerosene. There were no chandeliers, no piano, and no pictures on the wall. It was just a mean and ugly place to get drunk and get laid by a fat girl.

"Well, well! Look what the dogs dragged in tonight!'' Flora shouted. ''It's the marshal and his dirty deputy Haggen.''

Matt glanced at Festus and saw that the insult had its intended result; Festus's hands were balled into fists and his lips were pinched up tight like they did sometimes when he got real mad.

''Where's Nick?'' Matt said. ''I mean to have a talk with him.''

''I don't think he wants to talk to you,'' the big woman said, coming around the bar and marching over to block his advance. ''And I don't want to talk to you either, so you can just turn around right now and get your big butts out of my saloon.''

Matt took a deep breath. Flora reeked of her own bad liquor and a rancid stogie was poking out of the corner of her mouth. Every time he saw her she looked worse. He figured that she was going to kill herself sooner rather than later.

''I mean to see Nick,'' Matt said, eyes moving past the old woman and penetrating the smoke. ''Now, we can do this the easy way . . . or the hard way. It's up to you but I *will* see him before I leave.''

''You want to see Nick right now?''

''That's right.''

''Well, he ain't here. So why don't you run along, Marshal. Festus, you can follow him like the dog you are.''

''You're pushin' me too hard, old woman!''

''Bah! You're nothing but a dirty shirt holding up a tarnished badge!''

Matt cut off Flora's laughter with an angry frown. ''You tell Nick to get over to my office or I'll be back and I'll roust him out of here!''

Flora's cackle died. "You ain't got nothin' on my boy. He ain't done a thing wrong. All he wants to do is to attend his father's funeral and get what he deserves."

"What he deserves is a hanging," Festus observed.

Flora cursed and Matt had to grab Festus and propel him toward the door, and that's when Festus saw the other tall man who'd been with Nick. Festus hadn't seen his face, but he recognized him by his clothes and his build as well as by the gun tied on his hip.

"Say there," he called, "who are you!"

The man played dumb and looked from side to side.

"You know who I'm talkin' to, mister. I asked your name!"

"Why?" the stranger said, slowly turning to face the deputy. He stood well over six feet, was scarred, and was missing his front teeth.

"Answer him!" Matt growled.

"Name is . . . Smith. John Smith."

"Let me see some identification," Matt ordered.

"I got none. Don't carry my birth certificate either, Marshal Dillon. There a law against that in Dodge?"

"We're going to watch you like hawks."

"Buzzards with badges is what I'd call you."

Matt smiled but there was no warmth in it. In fact, it was a chilling smile and he leaned closer to "Smith," towering over him. "I know your kind, Mr. Smith, and that's why I'm almost sure that we'll be getting better acquainted if you don't leave Dodge City soon."

"You threatening to run me off, Marshal?"

"I'm promising we'll meet sooner or later," Matt told the mean before he edged past him and out the door.

Matt headed across the street walking so fast that Festus, who also had long legs, still had difficulty keeping up. "Matthew, do you think Nick will come?"

"Doesn't matter to me," Matt said, meaning it. "In fact, I'll enjoy dragging him out of there like a howling baby."

"Me, too," Festus said. "I don't know which of them two I hate worst, Nick or his ugly mother. How'd you figure that Mr. Dawson ever made such a mistake of marryin' up with some old witch like her?"

"Men do strange things when it comes to women," Matt said, trying to beat down his anger. "I'm sure that Flora was a beautiful woman when she was young, with a lot of fire. But she is the best example I've ever seen that people wear their living on their faces."

"Why, I guess they do," Festus said, scrubbing at another crusted gravy spot on his shirtfront. He was about to say more but the door suddenly opened. "Well, hello, Doc."

"Festus." Doc went over to sit down in the deputy's chair. He looked at Matt and said, "I did what you asked."

"And?"

"And I can't say one way or the other if Abe was murdered or not."

"Murdered!" Festus's eyes widened. "Matthew, you never said nothin' about no murder! I thought Mr. Dawson was already dying."

"He was," Doc said. "But the actual cause of death might have been suffocation caused by a piece of apple stuck far down his throat. I extracted it with a forceps."

"Could it have happened naturally?" Matt asked.

"Yes, but it's not likely."

"Doc, you're not helping me out here."

"I know that, Matt, and I'm sorry. For what it's

worth, I didn't see any other pieces of apple in Abe's mouth to indicate he'd eaten most of it. Also, the piece stuck in his throat was pretty old and I can't imagine anyone in their right mind putting it into their mouth, but Abe wasn't in his right mind there at the last.''

"Matthew, who could have done such a thing!" Festus exclaimed.

"The only one I can think of is Nick."

"But he's right here in Dodge City!"

"That's right, but we don't know where he was last night when Abe actually died. Doc, can you tell us when that happened?"

"I'd say Abe suffocated last night or very early this morning.''

"So that's it?"

"I'm afraid so, Matt. Sorry that I can't help you more.''

"That's all right. I appreciate your help."

When Doc left, Matt sat frowning. "It sure adds up to a murder, Festus, but I doubt we'll ever have any proof.''

"Well, you know them two Mexicans loved Dawson and so did his kids and Hannibal, so I don't know what to think.''

"Neither do I," Matt said grimly, "but when Nick walks in this door you can bet I'll mention apples just to see if I can catch him off guard.''

"But what good will that do?"

"If his expression changes, then I'll know," Matt said. "At least that's a start.''

CHAPTER

6

Matt knew that Nick would show up at the office because his warning was no bluff and Nick did not want to be humiliated.

"Hour is almost up," Festus said.

"He'll be here."

"I don't see how killin' Abe would change anything for Nick. I mean, he wouldn't get anything from the inheritance."

"Maybe all he wanted was revenge," Matt answered. "Nick is twisted with hatred and ruled by Flora. You know how much she hated Abe for tossing her out and then getting a divorce settlement that gave her only a few thousand dollars, barely enough to eventually buy the Red Dog Saloon and stock it with cheap whiskey and beer."

"Yeah, I know," Festus said. "I remember hearing about the day that Judge Blasdell ruled against Flora 'cause she was cheatin' on Abe with so many fellas. I guess she tried to kill that judge.''

"She did," Matt said. "She swore to get even with Judge Blasdell and all the other friends of Abe's that testified about her infidelities. I think revenge is what has kept her alive all these years. Abe was even afraid to bring his second wife into town for fear that Flora would attack the poor woman."

"It's a sad affair, all right," Festus said, "and the thing that—"

His words were interrupted as Nick threw open the door. "Well, well," he said with his lips twisted down at the corners, "so we meet yet again, huh, Marshal?"

"Afraid so," Matt said. "Come in and close the door."

"I'd rather leave it wide open. I got friends outside watchin' just to make sure you don't try to frame me."

"I don't have to 'frame' you, Nick. You're going to put your head in your own noose before very long. You always have."

Nick's smile died. "Speak your piece, Dillon."

"All right. First, I don't want you to attend Abe's funeral."

"Too bad, 'cause I'm gonna anyway. You can't stop me from it, either."

"If you set foot at the Prairie Grove Cemetery tomorrow afternoon I'll arrest you."

"For what!"

"I'll think of something," Matt told the man. "Abe disinherited you and your mother long ago and he wouldn't want you to spoil his funeral. Besides that, I'm sure that you weren't invited by James and Jessica."

Nick's face flushed and he hissed, "What them two want don't mean squat to me!"

"It does to me. Stay away tomorrow afternoon."

"Anything else?"

"I'll be watching you every minute," Matt warned. "If you so much as sneeze wrong, I'll come down on you like a mountainside. My aim is to send you back to prison with enough to put you away for life . . . or get you hanged."

Nick snorted derisively. "You and your jackass deputy ain't got nothin' on me and you never will."

"Why is that?" Matt asked. "Is John Smith going to do your dirty work this time around?"

Nick blinked. "Who's John Smith?"

"Never mind."

Nick started to leave but froze for an instant when Matt said, "Would you like to swallow an apple core?"

He turned slowly. "What'd you say?"

"You heard me. And I want you to know that I'm aware of how Abe died."

Nick forced a laugh. "Sure you do! Everyone knows the old coot wasted away with disease. Nice, slow death. Fitting, I'd say. My only regret is that I wasn't around to watch him suffer."

"Get out of here," Festus hissed, "before I forget I've sworn to protect even maggots and scum like you."

Nick dug into his pockets and flung money on the floor. "Here, Deputy Haggen. Buy yourself a bath, a shave, and a clean shirt. You're a disgrace to Dodge City."

Festus started for Nick, but Matt stopped and held him until the door shut. "Easy, Festus."

"I'd like to have a piece of him. I swear I would."

"We *all* would," Matt said. "And you can bet that, sooner or later, we all will."

It was one of the largest funerals ever held in Dodge City despite the short notice. Paupers, outlaws, thieves, and strangers were still buried on Boot Hill but those with money were either buried at Prairie Grove Cemetery or at nearby Fort Dodge. Abe had never gotten along with the army, so he'd preferred Prairie Grove, located northeast of town. Percy Crump looked dignified in his dark suit and half the citizens of Dodge were present along with several mourners that had traveled all night to be in attendance.

"This was a man of great vision, energy, and generosity," the Reverend Paulson concluded as the pallbearers eased the casket down into the rich, dark earth on cotton ropes. "And he will be missed by all of those present. Especially his dear son James and daughter, Jessica, whom Abraham loved more than his own life."

Matt and Festus stood in the huge crowd and watched as a young and obviously shaken James Dawson stepped forward carrying a silver trowel with which to toss the first bit of dirt into his father's grave. Matt heard several people sobbing with grief and James looked dazed. It was hard, but at least Nick and Flora hadn't made it even more difficult by trying to attend. Instead, they had rented a buggy and driven out and they now sat about a quarter of a mile away, watching. Matt had no idea why they had bothered unless it was to upset Abe's two children.

"And so," the reverend continued as James and his sister offered their last prayerful farewells to their father, "let us not grieve but celebrate this great man's life and remember what he stood for. Honor. Integrity, and perhaps, most of all—"

The sudden boom might have been distant thunder but there was not a cloud in the sky. And anyway, Matt recognized that the sound came from a big-caliber buffalo rifle an instant before James, who was starting to drop dirt onto the casket, pitched headfirst into the grave.

Jessica screamed. Matt and Festus spun around, eyes searching for the gunman. Matt figured it might even have been Nick, but it couldn't have been, because he was still sitting beside his mother in that buggy. People panicked and began diving for any available cover. Matt threw himself forward, crashing into Jessica just as a second shot split the air, missing her and plowing into a pile of dirt and sod.

"Everyone down!" Matt shouted, shielding Jessica with his body. "Stay down!"

But they didn't listen. Another shot and the Reverend Paulson was knocked over backward, the Bible in his hands sailing into the grave. People started running toward town and the noise and confusion were overwhelming.

"Festus! Do you see the rifleman!"

"No!"

Matt cursed because he didn't either. Because of a stiff afternoon breeze, there wasn't even a trace of lingering smoke on the horizon. With everyone screaming and running about in terror, and with all the places where an ambusher could find cover, it was impossible to spot the shooter. Matt crawled over to the grave and peered down at James. The kid had been shot through the chest and had probably died before he struck the flower-covered lid of his father's expensive coffin.

"Jessica, don't look down there," Matt said. "James is dead."

"Oh, my God!" she screamed hysterically. "No!"

"Stay down and don't move!"

Matt ran to his horse and Festus did the same. "Festus, I'll ride toward town and you make a big circle toward the fort. Arrest anyone you see trying to leave this area!"

"Yes, sir!"

Matt forced his horse into a run, quickly overtaking the funeral-party members who were racing toward town. When he got ahead of them, he reined north, eyes searching for something . . . anything that would give him a clue as to the ambusher's whereabouts. But there wasn't a thing on any horizon. He galloped on and on, but did not even see a spent shell or a crushed bed of grass where an expert marksman might have waited for his perfect moment to kill James and as many others as possible in the confusion.

Matt arrived back where Flora and Nick were still seated in their rented buggy. They were both smiling. "James and the reverend are dead!" Matt shouted.

"What a shame," Nick said. "Mother, isn't that just awful what happened?"

"Terrible," Flora said with a smirk. "I think we had better go back to the saloon and have ourselves a proper wake for poor little James Dawson and the reverend."

"Good idea," Nick said, waving good-bye to Matt as he wheeled their team around and started back to town.

Matt had never felt so helpless and enraged in his entire life. But what could he do? It was obvious that Nick had not been the ambusher but equally obvious that he and his mother knew exactly who had fired the big-caliber rifle shots.

"I'll get you both!" Matt bellowed. "I swear that you won't get away with this!"

In reply, he heard their crazed and raucous laughter.

They buried James and Reverend Paulson the very next afternoon, not fifty feet from where they'd both died. Few people came for fear that the events of the day before might repeat themselves and more would die. Dodge City was locked in a state of shock, outrage, and fear. People looked numb as they walked around town and both Flora and Nick were smart enough to stay out of sight.

"You've got to do *something,*" Barney the telegrapher said to both Matt and Festus. "You're the law and you're paid to protect us!"

"We're doing everything possible," Matt said as he prepared to return to the Red Dog Saloon and question Nick and Flora. "But I can't arrest anyone without some kind of proof."

"And what are the citizens of Dodge supposed to do until then?"

"Try to be patient."

Barney shook his head and clucked his tongue to show his dissatisfaction. "That won't do, Marshal Dillon. Yesterday, a boy and a *minister,* for Gawd's sake, were gunned down. There were other women and even some children out at the cemetery. They all could have been targets."

"That's not true," Festus said hotly. "If the man would have fired even one more shot, why, I'll bet that Matthew and me could have spotted him!"

" 'One more shot'?" Barney asked, eyebrows lifting. "And one more corpse? Really, Festus, you sure don't make much of a case. And I'll tell you both something else: If the law can't protect us, we'll damn sure protect ourselves!"

Matt stepped in closer to the man. "What are you talking about?"

"I'm talking about forming a lynching party and going after Nick and his mother! I'll bet they'd tell us who the ambusher was if we put a noose around both their necks and led them to a big tree."

"Barney, that's the second time that I've heard vigilantism mentioned and I'll tell you this right now: If anyone in Dodge tries to take the law into their own hands, they'll regret it for the rest of their lives. And if you don't believe me, go ask Judge Brooker how he feels about the matter and he'll tell you exactly the same thing. It simply won't be tolerated!"

Barney backed toward the door. "There's people in town talking a lot about it, Marshal. And if it gets started, you and Festus will be helpless to stop it. Two good people died out at the cemetery and this town isn't going to stand around waiting for more. Who knows who might be next!"

"Get out of here, Barney," Festus ordered. "We're doing the best we can."

"Do you even have any suspects?"

"Maybe one," Matt answered. "And we're going to question him right now, if you get back to your business and let us attend to ours."

"Well, Marshal, you had better come up with something quick, because this town is like a powder keg that is about to explode."

When Barney was gone, Festus yanked off his hat and slammed it down on the floor. "Doggone it, Matthew, them people expect too much too fast!"

"You're right, but we have to find that killer, and soon."

"Who's this suspect you was a-talkin' about?"

"That fella named John Smith we saw at the Red Dog looks like a bad one to me," Matt said. "And you told me you saw him and Nick together."

"Well, just for a minute or two. They might have been talkin' about the weather, for all I know."

"Let's start with Smith anyway," Matt said. "I'm also going to telegraph the federal prison and find out who else might have been released with Nick. Along with any names, I'll ask for a full description."

"You think that Smith fella just got out of prison?"

"I think that it's possible, yes. And, if they got out at the same time, we've got the pair of them tied together. Nick knows that he's watched too closely to do anything like a murder, but he could have hired that Smith fella to do the dirty work for him. I'll admit that it isn't much to start on, but it's the best I have right now."

"Then let's go," Festus said, picking up his hat and jamming it down tight to his ears.

When they arrived at the Red Dog, it looked just as it had the last time they'd come to question Nick. Same hard-nosed crowd and the same stench.

"Look what the cat dragged in today!" Flora cawed. "Marshal, you and Haggen come to pay another social call?"

"You might say that."

"If it has anything to do with what happened out at

the cemetery yesterday, then you best remember we were sitting in that buggy.''

Matt looked around the room. "Where is the one that calls himself John Smith?''

"I dunno.''

"Find him!''

But Flora just spat on the floor. "You want to talk to Smith, you find him yourself.''

Matt strode across the sawdust floor and stood before Flora. "I think I can find some building codes that are not being kept here or some other problems that would allow me to shut down this flea house for a week, maybe even two.''

"You wouldn't dare!''

"Flora, let me tell you something. Right now, if Festus and I were to leave town, I expect you'd have a vigilante committee coming in here to string both you and Nick up to the nearest tree or telegraph pole.''

"They come lookin' for me or my boy,'' she hissed, dragging an old shotgun up from behind the bar, "they'd best be prepared to meet Satan!''

"I'll shut you down right now if I don't see Smith.''

For a long moment their eyes locked in silent combat and then Flora finally looked over her shoulder and shouted, "Smith, come out here!''

A moment later the alleged Smith appeared. "Festus, take him over to the office for questioning. I'll be along in a minute or two.''

"Matthew, I wish—''

"Just do it. I'll be all right.''

"Yes, sir.'' Festus shoved John Smith toward the door. "March!''

When they were outside, Matt leaned closer to Flora.

So close he could smell her hot, fetid breath. "I want to tell you something in private," he whispered. "I want you to know that I am going to tie you and your son to those murders. And then you're going to hang."

"Ha!" the old woman cried, clenching her shotgun and taking a step back. "We didn't kill them two yesterday and you know it!"

"But you paid someone else to kill them," Matt said. "A boy and a preacher."

"Boy wasn't made of man stuff," Flora said. "He wasn't and never would be. Girl is just as weak. As for the preacher, this country has way too many Bible-thumpers anyway."

"You're going to hang," Matt promised. "You and Nick both. There's never been a public hanging of a mother and her son, so you will be quite an attraction. And when you are dead, they won't even want to plant you on Boot Hill."

Flora started spitting and hissing like a cat, so Matt turned on his heel and marched outside hearing her screech. When he arrived at the office, Festus had John Smith standing up against a wall.

"You got nothing on me, Marshal. I didn't do anything."

"Where do you know Nick from?"

"We met in an Abilene saloon."

"Sure you did," Matt said cryptically. "I'll bet anything you met him in prison and that your name isn't John Smith."

"Lots of people change their names."

"Maybe you're a wanted man. If so, I'll find out and you'll go to jail."

"I ain't wanted by the law. You can search high and

73

low and you won't find a wanted poster on me, Marshal.''

Matt had a feeling that the man was telling the truth.

"You know who fired those rifle shots yesterday killing two innocent people, don't you?"

"Nope. Marshal, since you just don't have a thing on me, I'd like to go now."

"Get out of here!" Matt snapped.

The man grinned and then sauntered between him and Festus. When he reached the door, he stopped and turned. "Must be real tough having everyone in town all upset with you for not being able to catch the killer. I sure am glad I'm not in either of your boots."

When he was gone, Matt slumped down in his office chair.

"Matthew, did you find anything out?"

"No," Matt admitted. "But I believe Abe Dawson was murdered and that whoever did it was connected to the shooting of his son and that minister." ·

"Well, I could see why Nick would want Abe and his son dead. And Jessica, too. But what did the minister do to deserve dyin'?"

"That's the same question I was asking myself," Matt said, picking up his hat and starting to leave.

"Where you a-goin', Matthew?"

"I'm not sure," he replied, "but maybe some fresh air will clear my mind."

"I'll be a-thinkin', too," Festus promised. "Thinkin' just as hard as I can!"

"Thanks."

Matt made the rounds, and when he passed retired Judge Homer Blasdell's house he decided that the man might be of some help. Blasdell was getting pretty far along in years, but his mind was still extremely sharp.

"Come in, Marshal," Blasdell said, after Matt had knocked on his door. "You look like you wouldn't mind a drink."

"Better not," Matt said, following the man into his spacious office, which was lined floor to ceiling with books that included all the classics as well as his legal library.

"What can I do for you, Matt?" Blasdell asked, sinking into a big leather chair and indicating to Matt that he ought to do the same with its mate in the opposite corner of the room.

In a few minutes Matt spilled out all his hunches and dead ends to the judge and explained how he was sure that Nick, Flora, and the stranger he'd just questioned were all tied to the murders. Blasdell listened with a deepening frown, and when Matt was finished, he said, "I didn't hear about that apple being shoved down Abe's throat."

"That's because Doc couldn't say for certain or not that it was murder. No sense in alarming everyone."

"Well, I agree with you that Nick, Flora, and that other man are part of the murders, but you're going to need some hard evidence before you can arrest them."

"I know that." Matt steepled his fingers. "Judge, you were one of the special few that were called to the Dawson Ranch to see Abe just before he died. Tell me what he said."

"He just wanted to thank us for our long friendships and loyalties, and then he said that he had bequeathed everything he owned to James and Jessica."

"That's it?"

"That's right. Of course, I already knew this because

I had drafted his last will and testament. In fact, I have it in my files and will be delivering it to Judge Brooker in a few days."

"I see. Who else was in the room when Abe said good-bye?"

"Hannibal and his children, of course. Then there was Forbes Montgomery, Bill Varner, Austin Sinclair, myself, and the Reverend Paulson. It was a very somber meeting, I'll tell you. One I'll never forget."

"I'm sure," Matt said, eyes distant.

"Why do you ask?"

"I don't really know," Matt admitted. "I have been thinking about when James was killed. He was the target and I think the second bullet was meant to kill Jessica. The third bullet . . . well, I'm not sure if it was meant for Reverend Paulson or not."

"I'd imagine not," the judge said. "I was there, of course, and it seemed to me like the shooter was just trying to kill people."

"You mean shooting randomly into the bunch of us?"

"Yes."

"I don't agree," Matt said. "Anyone good enough to drill young James through the heart at a great distance can obviously hit what he aims for."

"If that were the case, why would he kill the reverend?"

"I don't know . . . yet," Matt said. "But I have the feeling that I'd better find out quick. I'm going to talk to his widow."

"Margaret is very upset. I doubt you'll get much out of her and I can't imagine the reverend having any enemies. Matt, I really do think he was just unlucky. You

76

say that the second bullet was meant for Jessica Dawson?''

"I think so.''

"Then that's the question I'd be pursuing,'' Judge Blasdell said, reaching for his pipe.

"There's talk building about a vigilante committee going over to the Red Dog and hanging Nick and his mother.''

"I've heard about it, and tried to discourage it,'' Blasdell said, tamping fresh tobacco into the bowl of his briar. "But it doesn't surprise me.''

"I don't want to have to arrest anyone for murder unless it had to do with the Dawsons and Reverend Paulson.''

"Of course you don't. But people in this town are more upset than I've ever seen them before. If they do form a vigilante committee and start to take matters into their own hands against Flora and Nick, I wouldn't advise you to interfere. They're not worth dying for, Matt.''

"You say that? A man who spent his life upholding justice.''

"What happened to Abe and his son wasn't justice either,'' Blasdell said. "And you or Festus getting killed or hurt wouldn't be justice. Don't talk to me about justice, Marshal. I've lived too long to be lectured to.''

"I'm sorry. But I'd still try to stop them and Festus would back me all the way.''

"I guess I already knew that,'' Blasdell said, firing his pipe. "Just . . . just be careful.''

"You, too, Judge,'' Matt said as he headed back to his office, no closer to solving the murders than he'd been when he'd left a short time earlier.

CHAPTER

7

Nick motioned Charlie Roe over to the bar. "John Smith, we need to talk in private."

"Sure thing."

They found an empty crib and Flora showed up with a bottle and three dirty glasses. "Might as well celebrate," she said.

"We're a long way from anything yet, Ma."

"That may be true," Flora replied, lighting a cigar and inhaling, then blowing a smoke ring in the air. "But you got to admit that we're off to a damn good start. Two down and only six to go."

Charlie smiled. "I wish I'd have been out there when Moses drilled that Dawson kid and then the preacher. It must have been some kind of shooting."

"It was," Nick replied. "I swear Moses could shoot the eye out of a mosquito at a hundred yards. And just as quick as they were dead, he was on his way. Marshal

Dillon and his damned deputy didn't have a clue.''

"Too bad he didn't get Jessica," Flora complained. "They'll be watchin' her like hawks now."

"I know," Nick agreed. "We're probably gonna have to ambush Hannibal first. Then get Jessica later. Might be that she'll break and run away. She's been back to Virginia before and that's probably where she'd run to save her life."

"We could always track her down," Charlie suggested. "I wouldn't mind a trip back to the East."

But Nick shook his head. "If Jessica runs, she can have her life. It's the ranch that I want, not my sister's blood."

"Didn't seem to matter about your brother's blood," Flora observed.

"With a sister, it's little different," Nick said, knowing that sounded weak. Then he added, "James was everything to Abe and I was nothing. But Jessica was different. She's the only one of the lot that I'll spare."

"Could come back to haunt us someday," Flora said.

"Let's talk about who is next," Nick told her, wanting to change the subject.

"What about Hannibal?" Charlie suggested. "We could kill him next."

"We'll have to get him later." Nick scratched his jaw. "Let's get Forbes Montgomery. He and his fancy ways have always made me sick. He's rich as a king and probably has money stashed all over his house."

"You point him out to me and I'll take care of the rest," Charlie promised. "Maybe I can find his cash and set us up pretty good."

"All right," Flora said. "The high-and-mighty Mr. Montgomery it is. When?"

"How about tonight?" Charlie suggested. "All I need to know is where he lives and I'll do the rest."

Nick studied the man. "Charlie, if you're caught . . ."

"I won't be caught."

"But if you are, you're a dead man. If the town doesn't storm the jail and lynch you, I'll have to kill you myself."

Charlie blinked with surprise. "You'd do that?"

"Me or Moses the minute you spilled your guts."

"I'd *never* squeal on us! If I did that, I'd have to admit that I was there when we killed that old man up in his bedroom! What good would that do keeping me from a hangman?"

"None at all," Nick said, realizing that Charlie's logic was sound. "And as long as me and Moses are free, we got a chance to spring you."

"You wouldn't think of . . ." Charlie's words died.

"Of what?"

"Shootin' me through the cell window or something like that."

"Hell no!"

Charlie didn't look as if he were convinced but he clamped his jaw shut and waited while Flora poured them drinks. "All right," he said, nearly emptying his glass, "tell me where this rich man lives and anything else that might be worth knowing."

"Like what?"

"Like does he have a dog that might start barkin'? Or a wife that might start screamin'. And does he carry a gun?"

"Yes. Yes and yes," Nick replied. "He has a dog, a wife, and a gun. I know because I saw him pull it on a man once who insulted his wife. It's a hideout that he keeps in his coat."

"Is he any good with it?"

"I expect so."

"Are you gettin' scared already?" Flora asked, eyeing Charlie with suspicion building in her eyes. " 'Cause we got a lot of blood yet to spill before it all comes to pass and that ranch is ours."

"I ain't gettin' scared!" Charlie snapped. "I just want to know all that I can about this rich man. The more I know, the easier it will be to slit his throat."

"Kill his old lady, too," Flora snapped. "That Ursula Montgomery has always walked around with her nose so high up in the air you'd think she was tryin' to drown herself when it rains."

"Sure, Flora. I'll kill everything in the rich man's house and then I'll find where he hides his cash."

"Don't waste your time looking, because Forbes would keep it in the bank," Flora said.

"Well," Charlie argued, "that may be true but rich men carry a lot of cash around with them and often stash some in their houses."

"Just use the knife," Nick said, "and don't get distracted and then get caught. Is that clear?"

"Sure is," Charlie said. "Now draw me a map so there's no mistaking his house and let me do the rest without any more of your advice. And by the way, I can break open a safe, too."

"No explosives," Nick ordered. "That would bring Marshall Dillon and half the townspeople on the run."

"I know."

Nick drew his prison pal a map and then described the high-toned neighborhood. "I'd go up the alley," he suggested. "Maybe Montgomery leaves his back door open."

"I doubt that," Flora said, her voice starting to get slurred from liquor. "He might even have hired a guard to watch over the place while he and his wife sleep."

"Why would he do that?" Charlie asked.

"Because," Flora reasoned, "he might have figured out that we are killing all of Abe's witnesses."

"It will take a few more before that happens," Nick said. "Even Marshal Dillon isn't that smart and neither is his deputy."

"Dillon is rawhide tough and smart while Festus isn't nearly as ignorant as he looks," Flora warned. "Just don't underestimate either one of them."

Charlie went to bed alone for the first time since arriving in Dodge City and gave Nick instructions to wake him at midnight. When that time came, he sat up and rubbed his eyes, then yawned and muttered, "I'd like a pot of black coffee."

"And maybe you'd like a steak dinner, too," Nick said, swaying slightly on his feet from all the whiskey he'd drunk that evening.

"No, just coffee."

Nick didn't like it, but he went and brought coffee from the bar. After that, he studied Charlie as he dressed and made his preparations. "You're gonna have to do this right or we all go down."

"I know," Charlie told him. "We've already gone over the consequences."

"You got my map of where the Montgomerys live?"

"Sure do. But I don't need it. You said it was the biggest house on Spruce Street and just down from the

Union Church. Two-story place with a white picket fence."

"That's right. I don't know it for a fact, but I expect that Forbes and Ursula sleep upstairs."

"That's what I'd expect. Where does their dog sleep?"

"Either downstairs or in their bedroom. He's some kind of pedigreed thing that looks like it will run with its tail tucked between its legs at the first sign of trouble."

"We'll see," Charlie said, taking his Bowie knife from its sheath and testing its edge. "A dog doesn't worry me none."

"It should."

"Dogs can't talk, Nick."

"Maybe not, but they can bark and bring neighbors."

"You worry too much. You always did."

"One last thing," Nick said. "After you kill them, go ahead and ransack the house and try and find the money."

"Starting to feel pinched for cash?"

"Sure, who can't use some extra. But Ma reminded me that the really important thing is that the marshal and his deputy think that the murder was a burglary gone sour. We don't want them to have any idea about what we are really up to or any way to tie me into these killings."

"That makes sense. Don't worry, I'll take the man's wallet, watch, any jewelry, and whatever else I can find of value. I got a feeling that there is going to be a big payoff tonight."

"The payoff comes when the courts have no choice but to agree that I inherit the ranch when I present them with old Abe's last will and testament,'' Nick said. ''Then we'll all be rich.''

Charlie grinned and left Nick, who suddenly had a pounding headache from drinking too much of his ma's bad whiskey. He had a sudden urge to sleep, feeling sure that when he awakened late tomorrow morning, one more of Abe's witnesses would be dead and Marshal Dillon would be no closer to figuring things out than he had been yesterday.

It took Charlie less than fifteen minutes to walk from the Red Dog Saloon to the alley behind the Montgomery house. The house was impressive, for Dodge City. It was big and freshly painted white, with a fence all the way around it, probably for the sake of the dog. Charlie stood by the back gate and studied the rear yard, searching for the beast. He hoped it was outside so that he might lure it into his grasp with a piece of meat he'd carried in his pocket. But after ten minutes of waiting, he decided the animal was probably upstairs. Poor people's dogs slept outside, rich people's in their bedrooms. At least, that was what Charlie suspected.

Moving across the backyard, Charlie found a latched screen door that yielded easily to his knife. He reached inside and lifted the latch, then stepped into the kitchen. It was huge, with a giant-size stove, sink, and pantry. Charlie was hungry and he was sure that there were a lot of good things to eat here—but that could wait until he'd finished his bloody business.

There was a lamp on downstairs and Charlie recalled Flora saying that the Montgomerys might even have a night guard. But there wasn't one in the living room, the parlor, or the library, all of which were big and filled

85

with expensive furniture. He found one small guest bedroom downstairs but it was empty.

Charlie placed his foot on the first step of the stairs and slowly tested it with his weight. He'd done plenty of house burglaries and one thing he'd learned was that stairs were mighty squeaky, even in the houses of rich folks. But these stairs proved silent as he slowly made his way up to the second-floor landing, where another lamp gave off a soft yellow glow to guide the night wanderer. As far as Charlie was concerned, it was real neighborly of the Montgomerys to make his way so easy.

A wide, ornately carpeted hallway was lined with bedroom doors and Charlie knew that he'd just have to try them one by one until he found the master bedroom. And where was that dog, anyway? He sure didn't want to come upon it by surprise, because then it would almost certainly start barking and possibly even attack.

Charlie tried the doors one at a time. The first was locked. That was interesting. Charlie gave the matter a moment's thought and decided it must be an office where the rich man kept valuable papers and probably his safe and cash. Well, he was supposed to take care of the Montgomerys first and then make it look like a burglary, but a lot of things could go wrong and he wanted money no matter what happened. Charlie used his heavy-bladed Bowie knife to pry the door open. It wasn't hard. He stepped inside the room, and sure enough, it was an office.

Closing the door behind him, Charlie lit a match then found a lantern. His face split into a wide grin when he saw the old safe and knew that he could easily figure out the combination. It was funny how wealthy men got cheap when it came to protecting their money.

He crouched beside the safe and pressed his ear to the door. If it had not been for the need for silence, he could have broken the flimsy lock with a hammer and a good steel chisel. For ten minutes he toyed with the lock, hearing the old tumblers fall into place. To Charlie, they sounded like the dull and heavy clicking together of twenty-dollar gold pieces.

The tumblers fell easily into place and Charlie swung the door open, heart pounding with expectation. He was not disappointed. Inside the safe he found diamonds, emeralds, and other pieces of fine jewelry. Sure, he'd have to hang on to it until he found a way to fence the goods outside of Dodge City, but given the quality of these pieces, Charlie figured he could easily get two or maybe even three thousand dollars for the lot. He also found a magnificent two-shot pearl-handled derringer. It was loaded and beautifully engraved. Charlie held it up to the light, attempting to see the name of its manufacturer, and learned that it had been made in Germany by a company he'd never heard of before. The weapon was a work of art and he figured that it was something he would want to keep.

There were gold coins and some cash but not as much as he'd hoped. Charlie scooped them all up and crammed them into his coat pockets. He looked around the room, admiring other treasures less easily transported or fenced. Good oil paintings, a polished silver paperweight about the size and shape of a giant egg. It weighed at least three pounds and was inscribed to Forbes Montgomery, which would make it easily identifiable, and therefore impossibly risky to steal or keep in his possession.

Charlie balanced the paperweight in his hand and loved the glistening heft of it. Clucking his tongue disapprovingly, he slipped it into his pocket. Maybe he could file away the inscription and keep it as a memento of what was the biggest heist of his career.

He went through every drawer of the big mahogany desk, taking small items of value or interest and then scattering the remainder on the floor so that it would appear that the prime motive for entry into the Montgomery home was burglary.

Downstairs, a big grandfather clock chimed three times and Charlie was amazed at how much time had passed and at the lateness of the hour. He saw a chair pillow and cut it open to yank out the stuffing and replace it with more bounty.

It's killing time, he told himself. *Just a few quick slices across throats, then away we go, a much wealthier man.*

He left the bounty-filled pillow sack in the hallway and began moving silently forward, gently opening one door after the next until he arrived at the one where moonlight filtered through the lace-curtained window to reveal a sleeping and snoring man. Charlie paused, wondering where the dog and the wife might be. He decided the only possible answer was that they were asleep in yet another bedroom. Rich older men often slept in separate bedrooms from their wives, so that was not hard to figure.

Charlie drew his knife and slipped forward. With a single swift motion he cut the rich man's throat while at the same time covering his head with a pillow. The body thrashed and twisted, but it was confined under blankets and movement died as suddenly as it had started. Charlie did not remove the pillow to study his victim's face. He knew that the eyes would be protruding and that if the light were good, he would be able to read their terror.

Now the wife. Charlie exited the bedroom and went to the next bedroom. He turned the handle and eased the door open. Suddenly he heard a growl and then a deep, menacing rumble from the throat of a dog that sounded anything but afraid. Charlie fumbled into his vest pocket and found the scrap of meat he'd brought to buy the animal's trust. He tossed the meat into the dim room and whispered, "Good dog. Good boy."

The animal launched itself across the bedroom . . . and not at the meat, either. Its fangs bit into Charlie's thigh and he staggered, yelling in pain as the dog tore open his pants and worked its teeth deep into the muscle of his leg. Charlie slammed back against the wall and the woman screamed. For a moment he thought he might fall and that the dog would go for his throat, but he managed to push back into the hallway and kick the vicious beast back. Charlie slammed the door shut, hearing Mrs. Montgomery screaming for help.

His leg was a mess and bleeding heavily. He could hear the dog raising hell as it worried the door trying to get outside. If the woman had enough presence of mind to release it, Charlie knew that he would have no choice but to resort to gunfire, which would bring even more trouble on the run.

He scooped up the sack of bounty and hobbled painfully down the stairway, almost losing his balance and falling. When he reached the ground floor, he heard the dog coming down after him. Charlie forgot about pain and ran blindly down the hallway and out through the kitchen. He could hear Mrs. Montgomery screaming as if she had been killed and the dog raising a terrible ruckus. Charlie fell in the backyard, spilling some of the bounty into the darkness. There was no time to hunt for it, so he jumped up and ran for everything he was worth.

Lanterns appeared like fireflies and Charlie ducked into a barn, his chest heaving as he struggled for breath. Cursing men passed on the run and then Charlie slipped across another backyard and up an alley. He came to Front Street and crouched in the darkness, feeling waves of pain radiating up his leg. When he touched the wounds, his hand came away covered with blood. He would probably need a doctor to close these deep wounds.

No matter. The night had paid him very, very well and he sure wasn't going split all the stolen bounty with Nick and Flora. No! He was the one that had taken the chances and was now suffering.

Charlie took a deep breath and steadied himself before he stepped out of the shadows and headed across the railroad tracks toward the tough side of town. He'd done his job and the leg would soon heal. He just wished that he had been able to kill that awful dog.

CHAPTER

8

"Who could have done such a terrible thing?" Festus said with a sad shake of his head. "Matthew, we got a murderin' thief here in Dodge City. One who thinks no more of killin' a good man than swattin' a fly or mosquito."

"Anything you can tell us that might help, Doc?" Matt asked.

"Such as?"

"I don't know. I tried to talk to Ursula but she's not up to it yet. I did learn that she saw the man's silhouette, but that's all. I guess her dog, Fang, attacked him or she would probably be dead, too."

"That Fang is a man-eater," Doc said. "Vicious dog! He nearly attacked me when I came up the stairs but you're probably right about him saving the poor woman's life."

"We discovered that whoever did this was a professional. Professional enough to crack the safe and take all the valuables.''

"You know anyone in Dodge with that kind of knowledge and cold-bloodedness?" Doc asked.

"No," Matt replied. "I don't think Nick is a safe-cracker, but you can bet I'll be hauling him in for questioning."

"My guess is that he's not your man," Doc said. "I know him well enough to say that this isn't his style. Also, he's not stupid enough to rob a man and risk you finding evidence enough to get him hanged."

"That's what I told Matthew," Festus said. "When Mrs. Montgomery calms down, maybe she can tell us what was stole. That way we can watch out for it and get our man."

"There's something else," Matt added. "Mrs. Montgomery said she heard the killer scream when Fang attacked him. She thinks he was chewed up pretty bad."

"So I'd best be on the watch for someone with dog bites, huh?"

"That's right. And be careful. If you act the least bit upset or alarmed, it could cause our man to do something drastic."

"You mean like slit my old throat?"

"Yes," Matt said with a straight face.

Doc shook his head. "I can't imagine the kind of monster that could cut a sleeping man's throat. I just can't imagine what could do a thing like this!"

"Doc," Matt said, "you're a healer and still have a lot more faith in humanity than I do. I've crossed men that would slit *ten* throats for a few dollars and a bottle of whiskey."

"This has been a bad time," Doc said, looking upset.

"First losing Abe under questionable circumstances, then having James and Reverend Paulson ambushed at the cemetery. Now Forbes Montgomery is robbed and murdered. Dodge is going to explode if you and Festus don't come up with some quick answers."

"I don't think there is any connection between this death and the others," Matt said. "This one was robbery and murder."

"Yeah, I agree," Doc said. "But they were all murders."

"Maybe they *are* connected," Festus mused aloud.

"How?" Matt asked, turning to his deputy.

"I dunno. But maybe the same man that killed the others needed the cash to get as far from Dodge City as possible. I could check out the banks for anyone who might have brought in a bunch of cash or gold."

"Good idea," Matt said. "And we also can check the liveries and see if anyone buys a horse or buggy today. We should also keep an eye on the train depot in case our killer panics and tries to leave town in a hurry."

"We'll put such a tight lid on Dodge City that anyone leavin' will be like an unlicked thumb that's been stuck in a blueberry pie," Festus vowed.

"Catch this monster!" Doc urged with passion. "Whoever did this doesn't deserve to live even one more hour."

"We'll do our best." Matt started to leave. "Oh, and I'll tell Percy that we've got him another client."

"He'll want to put on a big funeral, but I doubt that Ursula will agree." Doc looked down at the body lying in a pool of crusted blood. "A monster. That's what we have loose now in Dodge City and I shudder to think who might die next."

Matt and Festus prepared to split up, with Festus going first to the depot. The next train was about to leave and Matt wanted to make sure that this means of escape was covered.

"Festus, if you see anybody . . . and I mean *anybody* that looks the least bit suspicious, then tell the conductor to hold up the train while you come and find me. Don't try to arrest the man yourself, because, if he opened fire, other passengers could be in danger."

"Yes, sir," Festus said. "Where you goin' first?"

"To the liveries, to make sure that no one is leaving that way. Afterward, I think I'll go have a look at the Red Dog Saloon and see what Nick is up to."

"He might be the one, Matthew."

"If he is, you can be sure he's not going to be hiding there. Flora will do whatever she can to get him safely out of town. We'll meet up after I stop at the banks."

"Be careful."

"Always."

Matt had no luck at the three liveries. No one had bought a horse within the last few days or rented a buggy or wagon. He didn't have any better luck at the banks.

Festus was plenty wary when he reached the train that was blowing its whistle in preparation for departure. "I need to have a look at your passengers," he said to the conductor.

"Is there a problem?"

"I don't know. You must have heard about all the murders we've had here in Dodge. Marshal Dillon wants me to check the outbound trains to make sure our man isn't escaping."

"We've only had six passengers board," the conductor said. "I know four of them personally because they are regulars."

"What about the other two?"

"Both are fellas in their middle years. Both traveling third-class coach and bound for Kansas City."

"Are they traveling together?"

"Yes, I think so."

"I'd better have a peek at 'em," Festus decided. "Did you notice if they were packin' guns or not?"

"Oh yes. They are pretty rough-looking characters, Deputy." The conductor pulled out his pocket watch. "We're due to leave in three minutes."

"You're never on time any other time," Festus complained. "Where are these two birds?"

"Two cars back. They're both wearing cowboy hats and outfits and they smell like they've been drinking."

"Probably nothing," Festus said. "But I'd better check."

"Who else was killed?"

"Forbes Montgomery."

"Oh my!" the conductor exclaimed, his face reflecting shock. "I've heard of him! He was pretty rich, wasn't he?"

"I expect so."

"How did he die?"

"Look," Festus answered, "I ain't got time to jabber about it. Especially if this here train is about to pull out. So just let me go about my business while you do yours. Okay?"

The conductor looked insulted. He turned and marched away. Festus wasted no time hurrying back to the third-class coach. This was the one where the local soldiers, cowboys, Indians, and generally folks like himself without much money a'tall rode. Festus had made a few arrests in this coach and he knew that his presence would not be welcome, so he removed his badge and slipped it into his pocket before entering the coach.

It was only half-full. There were the usual collections of above-mentioned men and a few women and children, which reminded Festus of Matt's orders to send for him if there were any hint of danger or trouble.

Festus pulled his hat down and shuffled up the aisle, trying not to appear too obvious as he checked out the collection of passengers. When he neared the pair that had been described to him by the conductor, he smelled their liquor. They were laughing and carrying on, using cusswords that they had no business using among women and children.

Festus halted beside their seats and glared down at them. "Gents, if you'll excuse me, I'd like to ask you a few questions."

The pair looked at him like he was daft. The larger one, who sat beside the aisle, snickered. "Who are *you* to be askin' us anything!"

"I'm Deputy Festus Haggen," Festus replied, pulling his badge out of his pocket. "And I don't much like your tone of voice nor your cussin' among ladies and children."

"Then you should just get off this here train!"

"No," Festus said, "I think that's what you boys ought to do."

"Huh?"

"You heard me. Now get up and start for the door before this train starts movin'."

"We ain't getting' off!" the other man shouted. "We paid for our tickets to Kansas City."

"You are drunk and raisin' a ruckus," Festus said. "You can take tomorrow's train after we have a few words. Now get up and move."

"Are you tryin' to arrest us?" the bigger one asked.

"I'm about to," Festus replied, hand moving nearer to his gun.

"Deputy, ain't you got anything better to do than cause us grief!" the big man bellowed.

"He can go straight to hell," the other added. "I ain't goin' no place but to Kansas City."

"Get up!" Festus ordered, drawing his pistol. "You're under arrest."

"What for!"

"For . . . for *refusin'* arrest."

"I never heard of such a stupid thing as this." The man started to say more but the train suddenly jolted forward, knocking Festus off balance. He had to grab a seat to keep from falling, and in that instant the big man was up and bashing him in the temple so hard that he collapsed in the aisle.

Festus tried to twist around but there wasn't much room, and then he felt his ribs burn as the man kicked him in the side and yelled to his friend, "Let's give him the old heave-ho off this train. We'll see how he likes cinders ground into his ugly face!"

They grabbed Festus, whose his head was still spinning, and started to drag him down the aisle. He had dropped his gun and still didn't have his wits as they threw open the door and started pulling him through the landing.

"Hold it!" the conductor shouted. "You can't do that!"

"Watch us," the bigger man shouted.

The conductor yanked a small pistol from someplace on his person. He cocked back the hammer and aimed it at the pair. "Release Deputy Haggen this instant or I'll shoot!"

Not surprisingly, they dropped Festus and glowered at the conductor, then turned and stomped back into the coach. Festus heard their laughter as he slowly climbed back to his feet.

"Deputy, are you all right?"

"Not hardly, but I'll make it," Festus said. "Stop this train."

"I . . . I can't."

"Oh yes, you can," Festus challenged. "Do it,'cause I'm about to arrest that pair."

Without waiting for the argument that was sure to take place, Festus took the conductor's gun, checked to make sure it was in good firing order, then slammed the door open and headed back up the aisle to see the smaller of the two passengers picking up his fallen six-gun.

"Drop it!" Festus ordered.

But the fool was drunk and rash. Instead of dropping the pistol, he brought it up and fired. Luckily, he missed Festus and everyone else in the coach who dived for the floor. Festus had no choice but to shoot the man before he fired again.

The women and children screamed and the big man lunged at Festus with a roar in his throat, but just as Festus was about to drop him in his tracks, one of the frightened passengers bolted out of his seat and knocked his aim off the target.

The big man crashed into Festus and drove him off his feet. Pinned in the aisle between the seats, Festus couldn't get his arm up to punch and he took a stunning blow to the face. He tried to roll, and when that didn't work, he kicked up with his legs, locked his heels around the man's head, and jerked him over backward. Freed of the big man's weight, Festus struggled up to his knees, ducked a straight right hand, and shot a left hook to the man's jaw that rocked him back and gave Festus time to climb to his own feet.

While the big man was fumbling for his gun Festus reared back and kicked him as hard as he could under the chin. The man made a choking sound and grabbed his throat as he tried to stand. Festus didn't give him a chance. Three more punches and his attacker was on his back again. Festus collected his six-gun and shouted, "Conductor, stop this train and take us back to the depot!"

The conductor yanked the emergency cord, and after several seconds passed, the train's wheels locked and skidded to a grinding halt. It took another ten minutes for the train to reverse direction, but by then Festus had his man handcuffed and waiting to disembark.

"You didn't need to arrest us," the man swore. "We didn't do nothing wrong."

"Then you should have made it easy on all of us instead of getting one of you killed," Festus replied.

There was a lot of confusion at the depot and the train was delayed nearly an hour until Percy Crump could arrive and move the body into his hearse wagon. By then, Matt had arrived at the scene. "What happened?"

"This and the one I killed were makin' trouble, and when I ordered them off the train, the other one opened fire, so I shot him. He tried to kill me, too."

"Maybe we got our men," Matt said, studying the

handcuffed man. "Why didn't you do as my deputy ordered?"

" 'Cause we couldn't afford to miss this train."

"Why not?"

"We was goin' to settle a healthy land claim back East. Our partners are gonna be mighty upset. Here are the papers to prove it."

Matt checked the documents and gave them to Festus, who read them then handed them back with a grim shake of his head. "Looks like he's tellin' the truth, Matthew. I guess I might have jumped to the wrong conclusion and maybe came on too strong."

"You're damn right you did, Deputy!"

"Now wait a minute!" Matt protested. "From what Festus has said, you men resisted arrest and Hank pulled his gun on Festus and tried to kill him. Isn't that right?"

"That's right, Matthew."

"Hank was drunk but he was a good man and he sure didn't need to be killed."

"He'd have killed me if I hadn't got him first, mister. And good men don't cuss in front of women and children," Festus said. "It ain't my fault that you two were so drunk that you resisted arrest and decided to fight."

"We'll see about that in court," the handcuffed man said. "I got a feeling that a judge will send you to prison and that you'll never wear a badge again."

"That's enough of that crazy talk," Matt snapped. "Festus, jail him then see Doc. You look pretty rough. Your ribs are hurting, aren't they?"

"The other one kicked me good, Matthew. Might have broken a rib or two."

"In that case, I'll jail him and you go see Doc right now."

"You sure, Matthew?" Festus asked, feeling worse by the minute.

"I'm sure."

"Did you have any luck at the liveries or banks?"

"No."

"Dagnabit." Festus drew a deep and painful breath. "Did I do wrong? Would a judge really send me away to prison and take my badge?"

"No," Matt said, shoving their prisoner toward town, "you did what was necessary to save your life. It's all right, Festus, he's just blowing smoke."

"I sure hope so," Festus said, looking whipped. "Things just haven't been goin' our way lately, have they?"

"No," Matt replied. "This is just about as bad as it gets, I reckon. Now find Doc and take the night off."

"Yes, sir."

On their way back to the jail, Matt was besieged by anxious townspeople eager to know what the latest shooting was all about.

"Is that him! Is that the assassin that's killed Mr. Montgomery or ambushed us out at the cemetery!" they kept asking.

"I don't know yet," Matt said. "Everybody stay back!"

"I say we get a rope and lynch him! We don't need a judge to tell us how justice ought to be served!"

Matt had to battle his way to the office and then slam and bolt the door. By then, his prisoner had lost all of his bravado.

"Marshal, those people think I'm the one that's been killing folks around here and I ain't!"

"We'll see. You tried to kill my deputy."

"I was drunk, but now I'm sober and I ain't guilty."

Matt could hardly hear his prisoner as he removed the handcuffs and put him in the cell because of all the shouting and carrying on in the street.

"Marshal, you got to tell them that I didn't do it."

"What about your partner?"

"What about him?"

"Did he kill Forbes Montgomery?"

"No! I told you! We were going to settle a land claim. Marshal, you got to protect me from that mob!"

"I will," Matt vowed, locking the cell and then heading for his shotgun.

He checked the loads, then took a deep breath and opened the front door. There were at least a hundred angry-looking people milling around on Front Street.

"Everybody listen to me!" Matt shouted. "There is no evidence that the man I have in custody has anything to do with the ambushing at the cemetery or the murder of Forbes Montgomery."

"Then why did you arrest him!" someone shouted.

"Just to question him."

"They say Festus killed his friend. Is that how you arrest a man for questioning?" someone shouted. "You must have more that you're not telling us."

"I don't," Matt shouted. "There shouldn't have been a shooting on the train, but the men Deputy Haggen tried to arrest were drunk and they were dangerous. Things got out of hand and that's the whole story. Now go back to your business."

"Too many people are dying in this town," Peeler, the saddlemaker, shouted. "Something is wrong here, by Gawd, and maybe it's time we had an investigation!"

"I'm carrying one on right now," Matt told them.

"And we will get to the bottom of all these killings soon."

"How soon!" a drunken and disheveled Texan shouted. "There's damn near as much blood being spilled here as at the Alamo!"

"Go back to your business and leave me alone to do mine," Matt bellowed.

"Well, you better get some answers pretty quick," one of the town council members shouted. "Or we'll find someone who can!"

Matt had heard enough. He backed up and slammed the door.

His prisoner was on his feet, hands clenching the bars. "Sounds like both you and your deputy are about to be unemployed, Marshal!"

"Shut up," Matt ordered, stomping over to his desk and sitting down to brood a few minutes while he tried to figure out what might go wrong next.

CHAPTER

9

Doc Adams straightened, then frowned at his grimacing patient. "Festus," he said, "you've got at least three broken ribs."

"I was afraid of that, Doc, and it couldn't happen at a worse time. Matthew and me is a-havin' all sorts of trouble about to break loose."

"What do you mean?"

"I mean," Festus said, "the townsfolk are going to be demandin' our hides if we don't come up with some answers as to who has been killin' everyone."

"I understand that," Doc said. "But you're doin' the best that you can."

"They don't think that's good enough, and to be honest, I can't rightly blame 'em. We got three murders and no arrests."

Doc wrapped the deputy's ribs with a strip of heavy

linen, then said hopefully, "Maybe the fella that you just arrested is a part of the puzzle."

"I don't think so." Festus climbed off the examining table. "C'n I go now?"

"You need to go to bed and rest those ribs. Keep that bandage on for a while. It will stabilize the ribs and make the healing go faster. And don't do any work, though I realize that the mere idea of honest labor itself is enough to scare you away."

"What do you mean?"

"Never mind," Doc said. "Just take it easy."

"How much I owe you?"

"Ten cups of coffee . . . and not yesterday's leftover poison that that you usually save especially for me."

"Aw, come on. You need to be paid just like everyone."

"All right, then, Festus, if you insist. That will be three dollars."

"Three dollars!"

"Sure."

"But, Doc! I once saw you dig a bullet out of a cowboy's behind and you only charged him two dollars."

"That's because he was broke, and with a bullet hole in his butt, he wouldn't be able to work for a month or so. With you, it's entirely different."

"Three dollars seems like a lot," Festus whined. "I only got about a dollar. I'll have to pay you when—"

"When you get around to it," Doc finished. "Look, just keep me in fresh coffee. Until things settle down in Dodge, I'm going to be hanging around your office more than usual and I'll be drinking plenty of coffee."

Festus nodded, relieved that he wouldn't have to pay in cash. Being overcharged by Doc would have been just another disappointment that he didn't need. He was already feeling bad, and it wasn't easy to pretend that all this trouble would pass and things would finally work out just fine. On his way back to the office, he happened to see the peddler's wagon that had shown up a few days back parked over at Delbert's Livery, sort of behind the barn but with just the wagon tongue and part of the front exposed. With all the troubles they'd been having, he'd forgotten about the peddler's earlier arrival.

"Better make sure he's not a crook," Festus muttered as he angled toward the livery to have a word with the stranger and to acquaint him with the city ordinances about selling goods. But the wagon was vacant and padlocked, so Festus guessed he ought to try to remember to come back and pay an official visit. Most traveling salesmen sold shoddy goods and fake cures at inflated prices but there wasn't any law prohibiting them from their trade . . . only the complaints that you heard from the fools that spent their money. Because of that, you had to keep your eye on these kinds of fellas just to make sure they weren't fleecing folks too bad.

"Festus!"

He stopped and turned to see Hannibal come riding up the street at a trot. The Dawson Ranch foreman's horse was lathered and his expression was grim. Festus forgot about the peddler. "Hannibal. Everything all right?"

"No," the old cowboy said, reining in his horse, "they ain't."

"What's wrong?"

"Someone is shooting pedigreed bulls out on the range."

"What!"

"You heard me," Hannibal said. "We've found three of them shot dead on different parts of our range and two more blooded bulls have been shot dead on Bill Varner's ranch. They've all been shot with what looks like a buffalo rifle."

"Well, what—"

"I think the same man who ambushed James and the Reverend Paulson is killing all our bulls."

"But why?"

"How should I know!" Hannibal exploded.

"Now simmer down," Festus said, surprised by the outburst. He'd never known Hannibal to be so upset.

"How can I simmer down?" Hannibal dismounted. "Festus, Miss Jessica is scared for her life and I can't say as I blame her one bit."

"You're keepin' a close eye on her, ain't ya?"

"Sure, but whoever this ambusher is must be one good rifle shot. What's to prevent him from sneaking up on the ranch house and killing Miss Jessica from long distance? Why, he could even nail her when she's inside and passing a window."

"I don't think that is likely. And besides, he'd never get away."

"Well, he sure did when he ambushed James and the reverend! You and Matt were there, too! I'm telling you, Festus, we need to find out who is doing this!"

"I know that," Festus said. "But until we do, you'll just have to keep Miss Dawson under close watch and—"

"She's leaving on tomorrow's train," Hannibal said. "I tried to talk her out of it but she wouldn't listen. Can't say as I blame her. Losing her father was bad enough, but then having James ambushed and killed at

Mr. Dawson's funeral has just about sent that poor girl over the edge.''

"Look,'' Festus said, "maybe Matthew can talk her into staying.''

"No one can,'' Hannibal said, looking older than his years. "And to tell you the truth, I think that she might be safer back east. I promised to go with her all the way to her aunt's in Baltimore just to make sure that she's safe.''

"Who will run the ranch while you're gone?''

"I got a good man named Wilbur Wallace. He can handle things for a couple of weeks. I'll come back just as soon as I can. Mr. Varner has also promised to help out if something awful should happen.''

"Hannibal,'' Festus fretted. "I think you'd better talk to Matthew before you and Miss Dawson board a train for the East.''

"There's been too much talk and way too little action on our parts already,'' Hannibal growled. "I respect Marshal Dillon a lot. And I respect and like you, too, Festus. But the time has come when I've got to do what I think Mr. Dawson would want me to do. Sure, the bulls being killed is a terrible blow both to our outfit and to the Varner Ranch. You know that Abraham and Bill Varner imported high-priced bulls from England to improve their Longhorn bloodlines. I'm pretty sure each one is worth at least three thousand dollars. But Miss Dawson is worth a whole lot more and I am sure her father would want me to take her away until this trouble is finished.''

"Sounds like your mind is made up.''

"It is,'' the foreman said. "You should see how hard Miss Dawson is taking the loss of her father and brother.

She don't eat much and she's down to skin and bone. The poor little thing jumps at the slightest sudden sound. Her nerves are shot and she don't hardly sleep. I've been bunkin' in the hallway right in front of her door just to make sure that she's all right.''

''That would explain why you don't look too good yourself.''

''Well, you don't look very good either,'' Hannibal replied. ''Someone whip you in the last day or two?''

''I had trouble making an arrest. Had to kill a train passenger that drew down on me.''

''He have anything to do with all these killings?'' Hannibal asked hopefully.

''I don't think so,'' Festus had to reply. ''And I guess you heard about Forbes Montgomery being murdered in his bed.''

Hannibal's bloodshot eyes widened. ''No! Why?''

''Wish we knew,'' Festus answered. ''It appears that he was being robbed. Mrs. Montgomery might have ended up the same way but her dog attacked the burglar and ran him off.''

''What is this town coming to?'' Hannibal asked, shaking his head back and forth. ''Can't you and Matt do something?''

Festus had to keep the anger out of his own voice. ''We're doin' everything that can be done. Sooner or later we're going to get a break and nab whoever is guilty.''

''Well, you'd better make it sooner,'' Hannibal warned. ''And in the meantime I was hoping you or Matt could come out and take a look at those dead bulls. I told Varner that I'd ride into town and ask. Maybe you could see some kind of evidence or signs that we couldn't find.''

''Then you looked all around?''

''Sure! Me and the boys even tied our horses and circled the carcasses on foot, hoping to find some kind of tracks or evidence. Varner and his cowboys did the same but none of us found a thing. Not even a shell casing!''

''Then I don't expect Matthew or I could either,'' Festus said, knowing how lame he sounded.

''Why would someone kill five pedigreed bulls?''

''That's a hard one to say. You'd think that they'd try to rustle them or butcher meat if they were real hungry.''

''Oh no! Whoever is doing this has it in for our ranches. That's why they're killing off the pedigreed bulls. This isn't about hunger or small money, Festus, this is about revenge!''

''Now, Hannibal, you can't say that.''

''Yes I can!'' Hannibal flushed with anger. ''The same one that killed James and the reverend is killing those valuable bulls, and I expect you and Marshal Dillon to find and stop this man! Both Varner's boys and mine are combing the ranch and keeping an eye out for anything that moves, but whoever is shooting our bulls must be half ghost!''

''Ghosts don't shoot high-powered rifles,'' Festus argued.

''Maybe not, but whoever is doing this sure can run and hide like no one we've ever seen. You didn't catch him after that cemetery shooting and we haven't either.''

''He can't keep getting away and we'll keep doin' our best, Hannibal.''

''I'm sorry to say this, but it sounds like your 'best'

isn't gettin' the job done around here. Now, I'm going to the train depot to buy two tickets so that I can get that girl out of this country until you do solve these murders. Don't try to stop me.''

''Why would we do that?''

Hannibal expelled a deep sigh and his broad shoulders slumped. "I don't know," he admitted. "What I do know is that you and the marshal had better catch the man or men who murdered young James, Reverend Dawson, and those bulls. Old Bill Varner is madder than I've ever seen him before. He's got his cowboys scattered all over the range trying to catch the ambusher and some of them are so jumpy they might start shootin' *my* cowboys by mistake!''

Festus clamped his jaw shut and watched Hannibal remount and then ride off to buy train tickets. *Maybe it is a good idea that Miss Dawson is leaving for a while*, he thought.

Moses Parker knew that he was running a terrible risk by still being out on the range. His horses were hidden in a stand of cottonwoods down by the creek, and twice this same day cowboys had ridden within a half mile of his hideout searching for tracks or any sign of activity. But Moses wasn't real worried. In the first place, none of the cowboys had a rifle that could match his own and none could shoot the way he could shoot. Because of the size of this country, the cowboys were scattered pretty thin and Moses was confident that he could kill any two or three that might discover either him or his horses.

He was hiding on the crown of a low hill, waiting for a particularly large Varner Ranch bull to graze its slow

112

and stupid way into his firing range. The bull and a few cows had been moving in his direction for the last few hours, but they were still about a thousand yards off and that was beyond even his accurate firing range.

And there was another thing that Moses was waiting for and that was the appearance of Bill Varner himself. Nick and Flora had given him a very detailed description of the second most successful rancher in this part of Kansas, and Moses was hoping to ambush Varner and send one more witness to the cemetery. Either that, or catch old Hannibal himself out on the range alone or with one or two cowboys that he could also kill. Any more than three, though, and Moses would pass; the odds of survival would become too long for comfort.

He was resting in a little hole that he'd dug out of the earth. It was really more like a shallow trench, being only about six inches deep and six feet long. But that was enough to hide him from view and allow him to drop a man or another pedigreed bull without being seen. It also afforded him a shooting position that was ideal. Anyone making a run at him on horseback wouldn't stand a chance and would die before they could get within a hundred yards.

The sun was warm and there was a nice breeze in the air, which was good, because it would quickly disperse any smoke from his big rifle. Moses wondered how things were going in Dodge City. He knew that Charlie had been sent to murder the rich man and his wife in his bed and then was supposed to make it all look like a burglary. Charlie had the easier job, while Moses was supposed to find a way to kill Hannibal and the owner of the Varner Ranch. Still and all, Moses had no complaints. The idea of creeping around in the night and slashing people's throats and killing women wasn't one bit appealing to him. It was far more challenging and exciting to play the role of ambusher. Use his incomparable shooting talent to pick off his victims one by one.

Moses smiled and looked up at the sun warming his backside. *Let's see now,* he thought. *We started out with Abraham and his six friends as witnesses . . . yeah, and his son and daughter. And now, thanks to me and Charlie, the son is dead, the reverend is, too, and Forbes Montgomery is most likely dead as well. That leaves only the daughter, her foreman, rancher Bill Varner, another rich man named Austin Sinclair, and . . . oh, yes, a judge. What was his name? Blasdell! That's it. Homer T. Blasdell. All together then the count was three down and five to go, if they had to kill the girl.*

Moses hoped that they didn't have to murder Jessica Dawson. He had a hard time with the idea of killing a girl, but it would have to be done if they were to get the Dawson Ranch passed on to Nick. Maybe she'd run and save her life. But for right here and now Moses was wishing that either Hannibal or Varner himself would appear on the range and that he could change the count to four down and just four to go.

He must have dozed in the warm sun because, when he awoke, the sun was getting low on the eastern horizon. Unfortunately, the bull and his cows hadn't moved any closer; if anything, they were even farther away. Moses frowned. He had spent all day in wait and in danger. The idea of returning to Dodge City without even killing an animal was not to his liking. So he looked all around to make sure that there were no cowboys in sight and then he stood up and started down the hill toward the distant cattle. Moses walked fast, and when he was within range, he sat down, balanced the huge buffalo rifle on his knees, then took aim on the bull. His finger pressed ever so slowly against the trigger, and when the rifle roared, he saw the bull crumple at the front knees, then go down kicking. The nearby cows hardly seemed to notice.

Moses didn't waste time reloading but instead wheeled around and began to trot back up the hill that stood between himself and the creek where his horses were hidden and waiting. He was almost to the crown of the hill and his earlier firing trench when he heard a distant rifle shot. He twisted around and saw two cowboys flogging their horses at him. One of the fools was shooting his pistol but the other was a little smarter and was trying to yank a carbine from his saddle boot.

Moses sat down and reloaded the big-caliber hunting rifle. It was a single-shot but he wasn't worried because there was plenty of time. He reloaded with smooth precision and then climbed into his firing trench and took careful aim on the smarter rider, the one who had the good sense to realize he needed a rifle. When he squeezed off the shot, the man with the rifle now in his hands flipped over backward and Moses saw the rifle jump into the sky and spin end over end before it and its former owner struck the green prairie grass.

The one with the pistol was smarter than he had first appeared and suddenly reined his horse to a stop, then wheeled it about and sent it racing away. Moses quickly reloaded, but the second cowboy was out of range before he could be shot. That was fine. Moses enjoyed killing things but he'd already just killed one man and an expensive bull besides.

He jumped up and ran down to his horses. Minutes later he was moving down the line of the creek, keeping in heavy cover. Just after sundown, he left the creek and headed across country. He would not ride directly for Dodge City but would angle to the west and find other tracks leading that way and join them so that his horses could not be identified by their hoofprints.

It was near midnight when he unsaddled his horses and turned them into the corral that he'd rented from the liveryman. Moses knew that Flora and Nick would be dying to know if he'd managed to kill either Hannibal or Bill Varner. He'd have to tell them that he had not but would keep trying, though not for another week or so. When news reached town that another prized bull and a cowboy had been shot out on the range, all hell would break loose. That was why Moses wanted to be right here in town under the law's noses where they'd never suspect him.

He felt good. There was a bottle of whiskey in the peddler's wagon and he'd have a few drinks to celebrate.

Still three down and five to go, he thought, *but time and opportunity are all on our side.*

CHAPTER
10

"Did you shoot old Bill Varner?" Nick asked the moment that Moses appeared in the Red Dog Saloon late the following night.

"No, but I shot another purebred bull and some fool cowboy."

"What good does that do us!" Flora squealed. "You were supposed to either kill Hannibal, Jessica Dawson, or Varner, not some nobody cowboy."

"I'll get them all sooner or later."

"You weren't supposed to come here, either," Nick complained. "Marshal Dillon and his deputy are watching me and they're asking about Charlie. You're the only one of us that ain't under suspicion."

"Well, ain't I the lucky one!" Moses replied sarcastically. "I get to risk my tail out on the range crawling with men looking for me while you and Charlie are sitting around this saloon. Is that it?"

"No, it ain't. Charlie killed Montgomery last night but got chewed up by the man's dog. He's in a lot of pain," Nick said.

"Well I'm not doing too well either," Moses said, his anger starting to get the better of him. "And if you think being out there on that range crawling with Varner and Dawson Ranch cowboys is any picnic, then let's trade places."

Nick had a hot temper and started forward with clenched fists but Flora stepped into his path. "Now, son. Moses has a right to be a little upset. He *has* been takin' the worst risks."

"Sure I have and I'm not going out there until things cool down again," Moses said with relief; he knew he was no physical match for Nick.

"That's a good idea," Flora said. "Nick, I think it's *our* turn next."

Nick stared at his mother. "What do you mean?"

"I mean that we need to take care of Austin Sinclair and Judge Blasdell, who both live right here in Dodge City. Charlie is lame with a bit leg and Moses is right about things being too hot on the range, so that leaves it up to you and me."

"I don't need your help, Ma."

"Yes, you do," she said. "And the main thing is that we got to make sure the next murder looks like an accident."

"How we gonna do that?"

"I don't know, but we had better come up with something."

Nick frowned. "What about that will we made Abe sign before we killed him?"

Flora made a face. "I been puttin' my mind to that

118

some and I decided that we'd best not say a word about it until all the witnesses are dead. Because if we did, we'd be showin' our hand to Marshal Dillon and that would be a mistake.''

"He's going to figure it out sooner or later,'' Moses warned.

"The later the better,'' Flora answered. She looked at Nick. "So we got to kill Austin Sinclair or the judge, and I say we ought to kill old Judge Blasdell first and then find that will that he drew up for Abe.''

"All right,'' Nick agreed, "but it won't be easy. As soon as the judge is dead, Matt Dillon will come looking for me.''

"And you'll be here looking as innocent as a sheared lamb,'' Flora said. "We'll *both* be right here with friends all around saying we never been out of their sight. We'll just act dumb and drunk.''

"Ma, why *act* drunk when you can *get* drunk?''

Flora pinched his cheek so hard that Nick yelped with pain. "Because,'' the old woman said, releasing her hold, "from now on, it's a game of wits and it's winner take all.''

Nick didn't like the idea of matching wits with Dillon but he knew that he and his ma, when sober, were a hard pair to beat. So he scrubbed his painful cheek and nodded. "Let's get the judge soon,'' he said. "Let's kill him tomorrow or the next day.''

"Patience,'' Flora said with a twisted grin and a cackle that caused the hair on the nape of Moses's neck to rise. "Patience will win this game.''

Nick dipped his chin in reluctant agreement and fretted, wondering if his mother was really serious about them needing to keep sober for a while.

"I'd like some cash," Moses dared to ask. "I sold everything worth spit outta that peddler's wagon and I need some cash to buy more goods to sell. Otherwise, it'll look suspicious, me being a peddler with nothing to peddle."

"You're right," Flora told him. "And you've earned a share of what Charlie took from the Montgomery place last night."

"He did pretty well, huh?"

"A couple hundred in cash is all," Flora said with disappointment.

"I thought that old man was rich."

"He was, but he was also smart enough to keep it all in a bank vault. Charlie said that he didn't even have a little safe. Nothing."

"That's a damn shame, but I still need cash," Moses said stubbornly. "We're in this together, and so far I haven't gotten anything but saddle sores for killing the kid and the preacher."

"You're right," Flora agreed, surprising even herself as she reached into her dress and found two twenty-dollar gold pieces. "You do deserve more. Here's forty dollars. Go find a woman and a bottle and enjoy the rest of the night. Then tomorrow, buy some cheap peddler's goods and stay away from this place. I don't want anyone to see you here. Is that understood?"

"I want more than a measly forty dollars!"

"Well you can't have any more!" Nick raged.

"I deserve a lot more than forty crummy dollars," Moses repeated. "Which of your cribs is Charlie hiding in?"

"Third one on the left," Flora replied. "He's feeling pretty bad because of them dog bites."

"Did you get him some medicine?"

"Now, how could we do that?" Nick demanded. "Mrs. Montgomery is certain to have told Marshal Dillon that her dog bit the man who killed her husband, so they'll be watching for anyone buying medicine or trying to see Doc Adams."

"Well, didn't you give Charlie anything?"

"Enough whiskey to keep him drunk."

"Dog bites can turn real nasty. I seen it happen," Moses said. "We got to do—"

"Listen," Flora said, "it ain't our fault that Charlie got hisself bit all to pieces. So just pay him a quick visit and then put it out of your mind and let's start worrying about ourselves. And when you go out back, tell my man that I said it was all right to visit Charlie."

Just as Flora had promised, there was a man standing out in front of the cribs taking cash and making sure that Flora's girls weren't cut or beat up. He was a huge man with a long handlebar mustache and a pair of arms bigger than most men's legs. When Moses told him that he wanted to see Charlie, the ugly bruiser didn't say a word, only pointed to the proper crib.

As it turned out, Charlie was alone. The crib wasn't much bigger than the poor tick mattress and crude bed that he lay upon. Besides the bed there was one table with a flickering lamp casting a sick yellow light on the thin, newspaper-pasted walls. Charlie lay buried under a moth-eaten old buffalo robe.

"Wake up," Moses said, nudging his former prison mate. "It's me."

Charlie awakened with a start, then peeked out from under the robe and groaned. "What do you want?"

"Money." Moses decided to run a bluff. "Flora said

that you had . . . fifty dollars that belonged to me."

"What?"

"My share of what you took from that rich man you killed."

"I don't feel so good."

"I suspect that's because you've been drinking way too much of Flora's rotgut whiskey, so don't expect no sympathy from me."

"No, it isn't that," Charlie said with a groan. "My leg is all swollen up and I got a terrible fever."

Moses placed his hand on the man's bare arm and said, "You're right about the fever. What happened?"

"That fool dog was vicious and he came at me outta the dark. I didn't see him until he had ahold of my leg. He sure took a good chew on me, Moses."

"I'll take a look." Moses drew back the filthy buffalo robe and then he took the lamp and raised it over the man. "Jeezus," he whispered, staring at the red and fearsome-looking bite wounds that were oozing puss. "That leg looks bad."

"I got to get to a doctor," Charlie wailed. "I could die!"

"You know you can't visit a doctor," Moses said. "Marshal Dillon would find out and that would be the end of you for certain."

"Well, what am I to do!" Charlie gripped Moses's arm hard. "Nick and his ma don't much care if I live or die. You can see how that is, can't you?"

"Yeah," Moses said, "I can see."

"Well, you got to help me! We've always been friends, ain't we, Moses? Huh?"

"Sure. We were friends years before we met Nick."

"Find me a doctor! I . . . I got a lot more money than I told 'em."

Moses grinned. "I figured you might. What else?"

"Jewelry. Probably all worth at least a couple thousand."

"Where'd you hide it, Charlie?"

"It's close. You help me and I'll give you half."

"Sure. But seeing as I can't get a doctor, I'll do the next best thing," Moses promised. "I'll break into Doc Adams's place and steal his medicine."

"But—"

"It's the best that I can do," Moses interrupted. "Now . . . now just lie still and I'll see what I can do. First, though, where's that money and jewelry hidden?"

"I'll tell you later," Charlie whispered. "Just help me!"

"I will. I'll be back as soon as I can. You got any whiskey?"

"Yeah." Charlie fumbled under the robe and pulled out a corked bottle.

Moses took a taste, which caused him to gag. "Holy hog fat! I've tasted better rat poison!"

"That Flora wouldn't give me anything better. She's awful, Moses. She's worse than Nick and worse'n us, even."

"Bite down on the buffalo hide so you don't scream."

"What—"

"Just do it!"

Charlie bit down hard and Moses doused the festering bite wounds with the liquor, sending his friend into convulsions of agony. Moses took another pull on the bottle then spat it on the dirt floor, saying, "I'll be back when I have Doc's medicine. Get drunk."

"I'll try but I'm real thirsty for water, Moses. Water is what I need 'cause I feel like I'm on fire."

"I'll tell the man outside to get you some."

"Thanks. Nick and his ma don't give a damn about me . . . or you either. It wouldn't surprise me none if they tried to kill us when we finished all the other killin' for 'em."

"I know," Moses replied. "That's why you need to get well and why we have to stick together and watch each other's backs. Nick and his ma are like a pair of black widow spiders, both of 'em real poison."

"I wouldn't ever do you dirty," Charlie whispered. "Not like them two spiders would."

Moses agreed that Nick and Flora would sell him down the river the first chance, or kill him. Either way, this was more than a game of wits, as Flora had just said back in the Red Dog Saloon. It was also a game of survival and that was a game that Charlie with his bloody blade and Moses with his marksman's eye sure did best.

Moses had little trouble breaking into Doc Adams's dispensary and stealing several bottles of medicine that looked promising. The old doctor could be heard snoring peacefully down the hall, but Moses didn't bother him and took pains to hide his entry or departure. If he were lucky, Doc Adams wouldn't even realize he'd been robbed.

It was nearly dawn when he returned to the crib. By then, the giant with the big arms was gone and the cribs were all dark. Moses was real tired as he shook Charlie back into wakefulness, noticing that the bottle of whiskey was dry.

"I got some medicine," he announced.

"Will it fix me?"

"Your leg will be as good as new in a couple of days."

"You're the only real friend that I have," Charlie rattled as a fit of chills shook him to the core. "I don't know what I'd do without you."

"I'll come back once a day even though Flora told me to stay away from her place," Moses promised. "Keep these medicines under the robe and keep still."

"I didn't get no water. Why can't I have some water!"

Moses heard rising hysteria in his friend's voice and it suddenly dawned on him that Charlie might get delirious and start screaming. If he did that, someone might tell the marshal and the game would be over.

"Charlie," Moses said, making a decision, "we're leaving Dodge City right now."

"Huh?"

"I'll be back with the peddler's wagon in less than thirty minutes. We'll head up the line for Great Bend. If there isn't a doctor there we'll push on to Newton, where I know they got a couple of doctors."

"I'll figure a way to repay you somehow," Charlie whispered. "I swear that I will!"

"I know that," Moses said. "We got to watch each other's back. Remember?"

"Yeah."

"Just hold on," Moses said. "I'll be back soon and we'll be on our way."

"Thanks!"

Moses practically ran to the livery and it didn't take him long to hitch up the pair of saddle horses that also served to pull the peddler's wagon. He rolled out of the livery just as dawn was starting to peek over the eastern horizon, and he drove right down Front Street past the marshal's office and then crossed the tracks and reined up behind Flora's line of cribs.

In less than five minutes he had loaded Charlie and that stinking old buffalo robe into his wagon. "Now," he said, "where is all that money and jewelry you stole from the rich man?"

"Right behind that crib I was in," Charlie answered. "I hid it under some old gunnysacks."

Moses found Charlie's bounty and threw it in with the man before climbing back in the driver's seat and heading out of Dodge City in one hell of a big hurry.

"How you doin'!" he yelled, twisting around to look at the feverish man.

"I'm not doin' so good," Charlie wheezed. "I'm feelin' real, real bad! I'm on fire, Moses! I need water!"

"We'll stop beside the Arkansas when we get five or six miles out of town. Then it'll be all right by me if you decide to drink the whole damn river."

"I'll never forget this," Charlie vowed. "I swear that I won't!"

"And I won't let you forget," Moses said as he forced the two horses east into the rising, coppery sun.

He drove ten miles east and then he pulled the wagon into some trees and helped Charlie out. The man was pale and shaky, with no strength at all. Moses could feel that his flesh was on fire.

"I never felt so bad," Charlie whimpered as Moses laid him down under the trees and then gave him a canteen.

"You'll get better. I'll go get that medicine I stole. In a few days you'll be as good as ever."

"You are my only friend, Moses."

"We got to stick together." Moses went to the back of the wagon and counted the money then studied the jewelry. Charlie hadn't exaggerated; it was all worth at least two or three thousand.

Not bad even if we get nothing else from coming here, Moses thought.

He doctored Charlie's leg but it sure looked horrible and there was a sweet, sickening smell that did not bode well for Charlie's future. But maybe the medicines would clear the infection up and it would all turn out okay. At the very worst, he had money and he was far enough away from Dodge City and that trouble to relax for a few days. There was some food and whiskey in the wagon and the fishing looked good. Moses had found a fishing pole, hook, and line and he well knew how to use them. This time beside the Arkansas would be well spent, but Nick and Flora would be furious when they discovered what he'd done.

To hell with them, Moses thought.

Four days later Moses knew that Charlie's leg was rotten with gangrene. If he'd been a surgeon, maybe he could have done something to save the poor man's life. But he wasn't a surgeon and so he knew that Charlie was a dead man.

"I got to see a doctor!" Charlie sobbed. "Moses, you got to take me to Newton or Wichita or someplace quick!"

"It's too late," Moses said. "I can't help you anymore."

"What . . . Moses! We're friends! Remember? We . . . we just got to stick together."

"You're finished, friend."

"What . . . what does that mean?"

"I guess you can figure that out."

"No!"

"I tried," Moses said with a philosophical shrug of his shoulders. "I stole Doc Adams's medicine and I've been taking good care of you since we got here, haven't I?"

"Sure, but—"

"I can't do no more and you're going to die," Moses said, drawing his pistol. "Better a quick death with a bullet than to die like you're about to die."

"Moses! Don't do this!"

"Sorry. But like I said, I tried and I promise I will bury you deep."

"Please, in the name of—"

But Charlie didn't have time to finish his plea because a bullet tore through his fevered brain.

CHAPTER

11

"Festus, let's sit down and try to think of what we have . . . or don't have regarding these murders," Matt said. "I've got a feeling that we've overlooked something."

"Mind if I add my two cents?" Doc asked, pouring himself another cup of coffee.

"Anything you can add will be welcome," Matt answered. "I've never felt so frustrated in my life. I know that it's almost impossible to commit a perfect crime, but we have three murders and not a clue. That's why I'm sure that we're missing something important. Some little thing that will help us solve this puzzle."

"Well," Festus said, "first there was the way that poor old Abe Dawson died with that apple core stuffed down his throat."

"Yes," Matt said. "But is Abe's death tied to the

deaths of his son, Reverend Paulson, and now Forbes Montgomery?''

"They have to be," Doc groused.

Matt expelled a deep breath. "Why?"

"I . . . I don't know. But they are, and I'd bet my last dollar that it all goes back to the arrival of Nick.''

"I agree." Matt went over to his desk and brought back a telegram. "I just received this from the prison authorities. They say that Nick was paroled with two others, whose names are Charlie Roe and Moses Parker.''

"Now, *that* is very interesting," Doc said. "Did they send descriptions of 'em?''

"Yes, but they're not much help. Roe is supposed to be tall and powerfully built. About six-feet-one and two hundred pounds. Moses Parker is five-ten and one-sixty with light hair and regular features.''

"That's it?" Doc asked with surprise. "That's all they said?''

"They're sending me old wanted posters on Roe and Parker so we can see their pictures. I sure hope that they send them right away.''

"Could be that is the key," Festus agreed.

"I sure hope so," Matt replied. "I have a bad feeling that we haven't seen the end to this string of murders. What drives me crazy is that I can't find the tie-in that would predict who is next on their list.''

"Hmm," Doc said. "I see what you mean. If it is me, for example, I'd like to have some warning.''

"Then what would you do?" Festus asked.

"I'd think real hard about boarding the train and heading out of town.''

"I got my own theory!" their prisoner called out. "I

figure everyone that has been killed is tied to that Dawson Ranch money.''

Matt turned to the cell. ''We've talked about that over and over, but we still don't see the connection.''

The prisoner, whose name was Dave Mitchell, shrugged. ''Well, if I was you, I'd keep workin' on that angle. Can't be any other than that they were all tied to that rich old man Dawson.''

''Forbes Montgomery was rich, too,'' Festus said.

''I think his murder was in no way tied to that of the Dawsons or Reverend Paulson,'' Doc argued. ''I think it was just a case of a burglary that went sour and ended up a murder.''

''I can't believe that no one came seeking medical attention for dog bites.'' Matt began to pace up and down. ''Mrs. Montgomery is just sure that her dog, Fang, chewed the murderer up pretty bad.''

''Maybe she was wrong,'' Doc said. ''Or maybe the guy was smuggled out of town and taken to another doctor.''

''That's an idea,'' Matt agreed. ''I'll send out telegrams to Wichita, Newton, and Caldwell. Any other doctors that you know of within a hundred miles of us?''

''Just the one at the army post, and I met him yesterday when he was in town and told him to be on the lookout. But so far, he hadn't seen anyone with bite wounds.''

''I'll get those telegrams off right away,'' Matt said. ''Now, is there anything else we can do?''

Festus shook his head. ''Matthew, I think we've gone over everything a hundred times or more already.''

''Then let's do it two hundred times, if that's what it takes to work up some logical explanation for all the

131

killings. Because if we don't come up with something, someone else might die soon.''

"Well," Doc said, "I did notice something very interesting today."

"What?" Matt asked.

Doc frowned and scratched his cheek. "Well, I think someone stole some medicine from my cabinets."

Matt had been sitting, but now he jumped to his feet. "What makes you think that?"

"It's gone! I had several bottles of medicine and some other little things and I can't find them anymore."

"Maybe you used them."

"Nope. They were supplies and I still had open bottles. I wouldn't have noticed, but I happened to be looking for some bandages and discovered the bottles missing."

"Any idea who could have done it?"

"Could have been most anybody," Doc said. "I got patients moving in and out all day long and I haven't time to watch 'em all."

Matt's shoulders visibly slumped with disappointment. "But . . . but was there anyone who seemed nervous or . . . Doc, help me out."

"I can't. I've been thinking about it on and off and I haven't even had any new patients whose names I could give you. I'm sorry."

"That's all right. If the medicines were stolen, that at least tells us that our man must be still be hiding in Dodge City."

"Matthew, there are lots of places to hide and we've already poked our noses into most of 'em."

"Well, let's poke our noses into *all* of them, starting with the saloons south of the tracks. That would be the most likely place a murderer would hide if he was still in Dodge.''

Matt looked to Doc. ''You got anything more to tell us?''

''No, but as soon as you get those wanted posters, I'd take them around to everyone and I think that is our best hope.''

''I do, too,'' Matt agreed, ''unless we can find a man with dog bites hiding south of the tracks.''

''We've already gone through every square foot of the Red Dog Saloon and all the cribs in back,'' Festus said. ''Nothing.''

''That's all the more reason why we should look again,'' Matt told him. ''If Nick and his ma think that we'd never return, maybe they moved the killer back to their place. We'll start there again.''

Festus nodded. ''Just say the word and I'll go over there right now and save you the trouble, Matthew.''

''No,'' Matt decided, ''we'll go together.''

Matt grabbed his hat and Festus did the same.

''Hey!'' Doc called. ''Festus, don't walk so fast with them broken ribs! You want them to heal someday, don't you!''

''Sure, Doc.''

''And Matt, don't forget to send my greetings to those other doctors! We're all sort of connected in this madness of medicine, you know.''

''Right,'' Matt called back as he headed out the door with Festus close on his heels.

They almost collided into Bessie Fife and Agnes Alder, two old biddies who were always stirring up gossip and trouble.

''Well, if it isn't Marshal Dillon and Deputy Haggen!'' Bessie cried, placing her hands on her wide hips and planting her feet far apart. "What are we up to this day?"

Matt flushed with anger. "If you ladies will excuse us, we have business to attend to."

"Oh, business," Agnes mocked. "It wouldn't have a thing to do with everyone getting murdered around here, would it?"

Matt leaned forward, jaw muscles clenched. "Agnes. Bessie. If you ladies have anything important to discuss, then get on with it. Otherwise, get out of our way."

"Well!" Bessie exclaimed in a huff. "Aren't you the high-and-mighty one! And what have you to say for yourselves after doing absolutely nothing to break the reign of terror that is gripping Dodge City."

Matt had heard enough and so had Festus, so they moved around the pair and started across the street. "Them two are sure a pain in the behind!" Festus growled. "I wish they'd leave Dodge City and never come back."

"Me, too," Matt replied.

"Marshal!"

Matt turned to see Nathan Burke, the freight agent, and Bodkin, the banker, hurrying forward to intercept them.

"You go on," Festus said. "I'll see what's on their minds."

"No, I better stay," Matt said, trying to beat down his anger. "Hello, gents, what can I do for you today?"

"Do you have any idea yet who murdered Mr. Montgomery?" Bodkin demanded.

"No."

"Well, why not! Marshal, do you have any idea how upset people are in this town!"

"I think so."

"I don't think you do," Burke snapped. "Because if you did, you'd have the killer behind bars! Maybe you and Festus have been in office too long. Maybe it's time for a change."

Festus pushed forward and poked his forefinger in the freight agent's chest so hard the man was forced to take a step back. "And maybe flappin' your mouth all the time is a-wastin' me and Matthew's time. You ever think of that!"

"Easy, Festus," Matt said, glaring at the pair. "I don't have time for this right now. We are doing everything we can to find out who robbed and murdered Mr. Montgomery."

"What about who ambushed Reverend Paulson and young James Dawson in broad daylight while you and Festus were present!"

"We're on that, too," Matt grated. "Now, if you want to talk about this any more, come by my office later."

He pushed on past the two angry citizens with Festus right behind. They crossed the tracks in sullen silence and entered the Red Dog Saloon.

"Well, hello there, Marshal!" Flora called. "And I see you brought your mangy pet dog this time."

"Where's Nick?"

"I don't know. Maybe with one of my girls out back. He's a grown man. I don't lead him around on a leash . . . like some people."

Festus bristled. "You got a sharp tongue and foul mouth, Flora. Matthew and I know that you and Nick are mixed up in something and we're gonna send you to prison or the gallows before we're through.''

"Tough talk for a little banty rooster who looks like he's been sleepin' in a henhouse 'cause he's so filthy.''

"Enough!'' Matt boomed. "We're doing another search.''

"That's because you got nothing better to do with your sorry selves,'' Flora said with derision. "But go ahead. Look under every bed and behind every box and cabinet. I got nothing to hide, but I do enjoy watching a pair of fools at work. Don't you, boys!''

There were about twenty hard-looking patrons in the saloon, but not one of them looked up from their drinks or said a word.

"Come on, Festus. Let's go through this pigsty with a fine-tooth comb.''

They searched and searched. Went through every room and then through all the cribs out in back but found nothing except Nick sleeping off the ill effects of another ruinous night.

"Ha!'' Flora cackled when they had returned. "I told you I was clean. But you can waste your time any old day you like, Marshal Dillon. You and that hound dog you drag around are already the laughingstock of Dodge City. And don't think this visit won't be talked about for days!''

"You mean old hag!'' Festus cried. "If you were a man, I'd—''

"You'd run for your miserable life, Haggen!''

Matt had to grab his deputy and practically drag him up the alley. "Festus, we've got a lot of other places to look and no time to waste on the likes of Flora.''

But they came up with nothing south of the tracks

after three hours of hard searches. Absolutely nothing.

Matt was visibly discouraged and so was Festus as they started back across the tracks, passing the livery. "Say," Festus muttered, "I just noticed that the peddler and his wagon are gone."

"When did he leave?"

"I don't know," Festus said. "In fact, I never even saw the man except from a distance. I kept meaning to go over and introduce myself and tell him we didn't allow any outright trickery or fleecin' of the locals. But I got so caught up in all the trouble we've been facin' that I plumb forgot."

"Well," Matt said, "he's gone and I've heard no bad reports."

"He stayed longer than most," Festus said as they continued on toward the jail. "Why, I think he arrived about the time that poor Abe died."

"What?" Matt stopped.

"Well," Festus said, frowning. "I seem to recollect that was when I looked out our office window and seen the man drive by. I remember he caught my attention because of that there bright-colored peddler's wagon he was drivin'."

"And it was about the same time that Abe was killed?"

"Yeah, I'm sure that it was."

Matt swallowed hard. "Festus, do you realize what this could mean?"

"No."

"I'm thinking that maybe this peddler fella was in cahoots with Nick and Flora and that other fella that we can't seem to locate. What was his name?"

"Smith?"

"That's right! John Smith—only we know that was a lie. I asked Nick and Flora a while back what happened to him and they said they didn't know. But . . . but maybe they *do* know and they're all tied up together in this somehow."

Festus frowned. "How we gonna prove that?"

"I don't know."

"I mean, the peddler fella and his wagon are gone and so is that John Smith fella."

"Maybe they're not gone after all," Matt said. "Maybe they're just in hiding."

"Where?"

"Let's check the liveries and start asking questions," Matt decided with more optimism in his voice than Festus had heard in a long, long time. "First, though, I'm going to send those telegrams off to the doctors in nearby towns. If we have any luck, perhaps that peddler put John Smith into his wagon and sneaked him out of town to another doctor."

"Why, that sure makes sense!"

"It's the only thing I've thought of yet that does," Matt said. "Check the liveries. Check any barns that are big enough to hide that peddler's wagon in case they returned. And ask every liveryman if they remember seeing the peddler coming or going or visiting anyone."

"You mean like Flora or Nick?"

"Yes, or our mysterious John Smith."

"I'll do it, Matthew, and it won't take but an hour or two."

"I'll meet you back at the office after I send the telegrams to the doctors and then ask a few questions of my own," Matt said before leaving.

Festus went to find Delbert, owner of the closest livery, and located him taking a nap in a little room where he slept at night. Delbert knuckled his eyes and said, "Sure, I remember him real well."

"When did he leave town?"

"Well, it was just a couple of days after Forbes was murdered."

"Did he say where he was going?"

"Nope. I woke up and his wagon was gone. But it didn't surprise me none, Festus."

"Why not?"

"Well, he wasn't doing much business in Dodge. I remember asking to look at what he had for sale and he said he didn't have much of anything to sell."

"What kind of a peddler is that?"

"I asked myself the same question," Delbert said. "And I hardly ever saw anybody come around to buy from him. Oh, I did the first few days but then he just sort of stopped doing business. I guess he gave up on folks around here and headed for greener pastures."

Festus scowled. "I only saw him from a distance one time. What'd he look like?"

"Sorta ordinary. Seemed real pleasant but he kept to himself."

"Did you ever see him go over to the Red Dog Saloon or around town with Nick or Flora?"

"Nope. Like I said, he was a loner. I think he slept a lot in the day and I don't ask nor do I care what he did at night. Might have played cards or whored for all I know."

"Gimme a description of the fella."

"Hmm, I'd say he was about your height and build. Had lighter hair and was cleaner . . . no offense."

"None taken," Festus growled. "What else?"

"I can't recall anything else."

"Come on, Delbert! You've got to think of something. What you gave me fits half the men in Dodge City, or Kansas itself, for that matter."

"I'm sorry, but he was real ordinary. Seemed pleasant enough. Had a nice, friendly smile."

"Did he wear a gun?"

"Yeah, a pistol."

"Any scars or anything?"

"Nope."

"You're not much help," Festus complained.

"Well, excuse me!" Delbert climbed off his bunk and stuffed his shirt into his baggy pants. "I got better things to do than get insulted by you, Festus."

"Look, if you can think of anything else about him, let me know, all right?"

"Sure!"

"And I'll bring by a wanted poster as soon as it arrives. Maybe then you'll remember a little more about this fella."

"Don't count on it."

Festus went to the other two liveries and peeked into every barn in Dodge City. When he returned to the office, he told Matt what he'd found out and said, "I know it ain't much help but that's all I could get out of Delbert."

"I sure hope those wanted posters arrive soon," Matt said. "It seems like we can't do much more than wait on them."

"I know," Festus said. "Do you think the peddler and that John Smith were released from prison with Nick?"

"I'd almost bet on it," Matt replied. "If they weren't, we've gone up yet another blind alley."

"Maybe you should take tomorrow off and go fishing," Festus suggested.

"What!"

"I'm serious. You need some time off."

"Yeah, but that would be about the last straw," Matt said. "Day after tomorrow, I'd be looking for a new job and so would you."

"We could find new jobs in another town, maybe even better ones."

"Uh-uh," Matt said. "I've grown attached to this place and its people. I'm not ready to start all over."

"Maybe it's Miss Kitty that keeps you here," Festus said.

"Aw, go take a walk or a nap," Matt snapped, then looked out the window and saw Hannibal and Miss Dawson coming up the street, apparently on their way to the train depot. "I'd better say good-bye to Jessica Dawson."

Matt caught up with them at the train depot. True to Hannibal's description, the young woman looked thin and distressed. "Miss Dawson, I just wanted to say that I'm sorry we haven't been able to catch your brother's killer."

"Whoever killed him killed my father," she said. "You won't give up on this, will you, Marshal?"

"Never."

"Thank you."

"Are you coming back?"

"I . . . I just don't know. The ranch is in capable hands now and I need some time away to . . . to just feel better. All these murders and everything!"

Matt swallowed. "Look," he said, "there is an explanation for all of this and I'm going to find it, so help me God."

"Just be careful. You, too, Hannibal!"

The ranch foreman smiled. "Don't worry about me. I've got nothing of value, so I'm safe."

"I hope so," Jessica said as the train whistle blew and the conductor shouted, "All aboard!"

Matt and Hannibal waited until the train pulled out, going east, and then they walked over to the buggy. "Matt, she's a fine girl and doesn't deserve all this tragedy."

"I know. Take care of yourself, Hannibal."

"I will. See you soon, Matt. Keep us posted about what is going on."

"I sure will," Matt promised.

And then Hannibal climbed into the buggy and headed off to the Dawson Ranch.

CHAPTER

12

"So," Flora said as she and Nick watched the wagon leave Dodge and head north, "there goes Hannibal back to the Dawson Ranch and Miss Jessica has gone back east on the train."

"I'm glad," Nick said. "I didn't want to kill her. She's the only one of the bunch that never looked down their nose at me."

"You've always been smitten with Abe's daughter," Flora said scornfully. "But Jessica was weak and unworthy."

Nick started to protest but Flora interrupted. "Let's not talk about her. I'm thinking that we need to do something about Hannibal."

"Now?"

"When would we ever have a better chance to kill him?"

"I . . . I thought we were going after Sinclair next."

"Maybe you can do him after Hannibal tonight."

"Ma, I don't know. The town is upset as it is, and two more killings would blow the lid off Dodge."

"Then let it blow!" Flora howled. "The most likely thing that will happen is the townspeople will be so upset they'll insist the town council fire Matt Dillon. And wouldn't that be just perfect?"

"I hadn't thought about it," Nick admitted.

"Well, I have. With Dillon out of the picture, things will be easier all the way around. Much easier."

"Do you really think they'd get rid of him?"

"Yes," Flora declared. "We could start a petition and put a fire under the town council, if needed. But I'm thinking that we wouldn't have to do much more than sit back and watch the fireworks."

"Killing another man would be risky for me, Ma."

"I know that, and I'm going to give Moses and Charlie a lot of trouble for taking off without a word of why or where. What kind of friends do you have, anyway?"

"They've done all that's been asked of them so far," Nick said defensively. "And it was a good thing that they weren't here when Dillon and Haggen came back for another search. What would have happened if they'd have found Charlie with that festering leg out back?"

"We'd have been in real trouble, but they still couldn't have proved we were in cahoots."

"They could have if Charlie would have talked. He was feverish enough that I expect he would have sang like a mockingbird. Ma, we owe Moses plenty for taking Charlie off somewhere."

"Maybe. But with the both of 'em gone, that sort of just leaves us to do what's left of the dirty work, starting with Hannibal."

"I could get a horse and overtake him," Nick said. "That would be easy enough."

"Could you make it look like an accident?"

"How?"

Flora scowled. "I don't know."

"It wouldn't wash, Ma. No one would believe that Hannibal would just topple out of his wagon and bust his neck."

"I suppose not."

"I'll just have to shoot him," Nick decided, checking his six-gun.

"Then go do it, son. We might never have this good a chance again."

Nick headed out the back way. In less than five minutes he was galloping north with the dying sun burnishing the long green grass. He rode hard, but Hannibal was also pushing his team, so it took nearly an hour to circle around and then come riding south toward the ranch foreman, with his hat pulled low so that the older man couldn't see his face until they were close.

"Hello there!" Hannibal called. "Where you headed, stranger?"

In reply, Nick reached under his coat and drew out his six-gun. Tipping his hat brim back with the barrel of his pistol, he said, "I'm headed for Dodge City. The more interesting question is, where are you headed?"

Too late did Hannibal recognize Nick and claw for his gun. Three bullets struck him in the chest before he could clear his holster. Hannibal pitched over his seat and the team of horses bolted into a run, heading for their home ranch.

"So long," Nick said, tipping his hat to the runaway

team and a man that had never liked or helped him much when he'd been a boy.

It was way past dark when Nick slipped unnoticed back into the Red Dog Saloon. Flora had been anxiously watching and waiting for his arrival and she took his arm and they went back to her office, walking a little unsteadily because of the drink.

"Well?" she asked.

"Hannibal is dead."

"No problems?"

"None." Nick giggled. "Ma, you should have seen that old man's face when I raised my hat and he recognized who I was! I swear he turned about five shades of white and his eyes got as big as silver dollars. I shot him three times in the heart and the last I saw, his body was headed north."

"Did you make sure he was dead?"

"He was dead, all right. I didn't need to take his pulse, Ma."

Flora expelled a deep breath of relief. "Good boy! Now it's Austin Sinclair's turn."

"I think I should kill Judge Blasdell tonight, then find and destroy Abe's original will."

Flora gave the matter some consideration then dipped her chin, saying, "I guess that would be better. All right. I always hated Blasdell anyway."

"He's as good as dead," Nick vowed. "Then the only witnesses left will be Bill Varner and Austin Sinclair."

"I hope Moses shows up in time to get 'em," Flora replied. "It's awful risky for you to be out with Marshal Dillon watching us so close. That's why we need to get him tossed out of office. If that fool Haggen takes his place, so much the better.''

"He's not as stupid as he looks," Nick warned.

"Yeah, but he's not as smart as Dillon, either.''

"That's true.''

"How are you going to get the judge tonight?''

"He lives alone, don't he?''

"I think so.''

"Then what's the problem?''

"I hear he always carries a gun for protection because he's sent so many men to prison or the gallows.''

"Hannibal wore a gun and it didn't help him much.''

Flora grinned and then fished a bottle out of her desk drawer. Uncorking it, she took several long swallows, then started to cork and return it, but Nick said, "That's the best stuff in the house, ain't it?''

"Yes, but—''

"I guess I deserve a good taste for killing Hannibal and for what I'm about to do to the judge.''

"Just a small taste," Flora cautioned. "You got to be clearheaded when you go after Blasdell.''

"You worry way too much, Ma.''

Her bloodshot eyes misted. "What do you expect? You're my only child. You're all I got in the world now.''

Nick took a pull on the bottle and pounded the cork in deep. "Ma," he said, "when I inherit the Dawson Ranch, you and me are going to live awful good. Better than ever before. And the people who been looking down at us all these years will have to eat crow. We'll have more money than we know what to do with and we can have our way in this town.''

"I don't want to live way out there on a ranch. I like it here just fine."

"Then I'll build you a saloon better than the Long Branch and you can show that high-and-mighty Miss Kitty Russell a thing or two."

"Aw, Kitty ain't so bad. She never said a bad word to me."

"Maybe not to your face."

"You're right," Flora said. "She's probably as bad as all the rest who try to pass as respectable women. Anyway, just be careful and try to make it look like you robbed Judge Blasdell and then had to kill him."

"I see. That way they'll think it was the same man who robbed Montgomery."

"That's right."

"You're real smart, Ma."

"When you're a woman in the West, you'd better be smart or men will take you down and you'll wind up old and ugly and poor."

"Well, you got this saloon and the rest. You did good even after Dawson threw you out."

Flora's eyes blazed. "He didn't 'throw me out'! I walked out on my own! It was me that left Abraham, not the other way around."

"Yeah," Nick said, not believing a word of it. "I better go get ready to pay the judge a visit."

"Be careful. Charlie probably figured he'd have an easy time killin' Montgomery, but things can go wrong. I don't want anything to happen to you, son. It'd . . . well, it'd break my poor old heart."

Her eyes filled with tears and she uncorked the bottle and drank some more whiskey. Nick knew his ma was about to get weepy, so he patted her on the arm and hurried off to kill Judge Blasdell.

The old man lived in a roomy but modest house over on First Avenue. Nick had even been in the place a time or two in his younger days when Blasdell had summoned him in for a good reprimand in the hopes of turning him into a solid citizen. That helped, because he remembered the general layout of the house and knew where the judge slept. Blasdell's wife had died about five years before, wasted away with some awful disease that had made her howl with pain like an animal. Nick recalled how Doc Adams had been summoned over about every few hours during Mrs. Blasdell's last days to give the poor woman laudanum. As far as Nick was concerned, he'd rather hang or get shot than die slow that way.

The house was dark and Nick crouched under a tree in the backyard, studying the place and wondering if the judge also had a dog that might attack an intruder like the Montgomery dog had chewed up poor Charlie. He couldn't recall the judge having a dog back then, but that didn't mean he hadn't gotten one since. Nick hoped Judge Blasdell had settled for a cat instead.

He left the dark shadows under the tree and made his way directly to the back door. It was locked, but that came as no problem because Nick carried a pry bar. It didn't take long to jimmy the door open and slip inside. He lit a match, got his bearings, and tiptoed toward the judge's bedroom, the door of which was wide open. Unfortunately, a board creaked loudly under the flooring and Nick froze on the threshold.

"Judge!" a woman whispered. "Judge, someone is in this house! Judge!"

Nick drew in a sharp breath and heard old Blasdell mutter something unintelligible. He hoped the pair would go back to sleep in a few minutes.

"Judge, wake up!"

Whispered voices. The creaking of bedsprings and then the protest of floorboards. Nick could feel sweat beginning to trickle down his spine. The very last thing he'd expected was for the judge to be sleeping with some woman.

"Mildred, I didn't hear anything."

"That's because you were snoring! Homer, I swear there is someone in this house!"

More muttering. "All right. All right! I'll look around."

Nick was caught in a dilemma. If he retreated, the judge would probably hear his movements because of the loose floor. But if he didn't retreat, he'd be caught flat-footed in the living room.

He had to reach a quick decision and so he drew his gun, praying that he would not have to use it and bring neighbors running.

"Who goes there!" Judge Blasdell demanded.

Nick raised the barrel of his pistol. He couldn't see the judge's face but he sure recognized his voice. "Freeze, Judge! This is a robbery."

"The hell you say!"

Nick didn't see the small pistol until it spat flame and then he felt its fire sear across his arm. He staggered and returned fire. The judge grunted and sat down hard, but he shot again and Nick swore he could hear the bullet whine past his right ear.

"Help!" the woman screamed. "Oh, my God!"

Nick shot again and the dark silhouette of the judge slumped to the floor. But the woman was out of the bed and snatching up the little handgun. "You're not going to slit our throats!" she cried, opening fire and hitting Nick in the hand.

"Ahhh!" he groaned as his six-gun clattered to the floor. He turned tail and ran for his life with the sound of barking dogs and screaming neighbors filling his ears.

It was a miracle that he managed to get out of the neighborhood alive and then back to the Red Dog Saloon without being seen. When he burst in through the back door, he looked down and saw that blood was pouring from his right hand and that his little finger was partially missing. "Doggone!" he cursed, grabbing a rag and trying to stop the bleeding.

Flora was at his side instantly, and for a moment she thought she was going to faint. "You've been shot!"

"That's right, but I'll live . . . probably just long enough to hang."

"What went wrong!"

"He had a woman, Ma. She heard me, and when I shot the judge, she picked up his handgun and opened fire. It was the last thing I expected."

"Did you kill old Blasdell?"

"I can't say, but probably."

"What about the will?"

"I never had time to look for it. I was too busy trying to stay alive."

"We've got to get you out of here. Dillon is going to be coming 'round soon, and when he sees that hand he's going to arrest you for murder."

"Where can I hide?"

Flora clasped her head in her hands. "Let me see. I know. Do you remember where we used to go fishin' on Sundays while everyone else was in church?"

"Sure."

"And remember that little cave under them bushes. The one that looked like—"

"I remember!"

"Go there now."

"What about my hand, Ma!"

"Let me see."

Flora examined the wound and gulped, then said, "It's not that bad."

"Ma, my finger is mostly shot off!"

"Yeah, but how does that compare to a stretched neck?"

Nick got the message. "All right. All right," he said breathlessly. "I'll go there and hide. Will you send someone out to get me?"

"I will, but not until it's safe. We got to find you a safe place outside town to hide until that hand heals. But for now, I'll send food and bandages."

"And whiskey, Ma. I need some right now."

"There's no time," she said. "Now git! And don't you try to leave that little cave until I send word for you to come. Hear me?"

"Ma, there's only Varner and Sinclair left to kill. You can hire someone to finish them off, can't you? I could go away for a month or two and then come back and make my claim on the ranch. That'd work, wouldn't it?"

"Of course it would! Now hurry off and don't let anyone see you headin' for the river."

"Whiskey," he choked. "It's already hurting something terrible, Ma."

She disappeared, then returned with two bottles, saying, "Don't you start to drinkin' until you're safe in hiding."

"I won't. I don't want to get caught and hanged."

"I should have never let you go. Damn Charlie and Moses! They're the ones that should be runnin' and hidin' right now. Not my boy!"

They hugged, and despite himself, Nick sobbed with his pain and fear, shedding hot tears just like his ma.

"Hurry off now before Dillon comes around. When they find out the judge is dead, all hell is going to break loose the likes of which has never been seen in Dodge City and never will be again!"

Nick shot out the back door and ran down the alley figuring that was the gospel truth.

CHAPTER

1 3

When Matt and Festus arrived at the judge's house, Doc Adams was desperately trying to save his old friend's life.

"Doc!" Matt whispered, kneeling down beside the judge. "What are his chances?"

"Slim to none," Doc replied with bitterness. "Homer took two bullets and he's dying."

Matt shook his head. "Who would do this?"

"I guess that's the question we're all asking and the one you need to answer," Doc snapped just as Judge Blasdell shivered and then emptied his lungs for the last time.

Matt had known and respected the judge for many years; it was several moments before he could ask, "Doc, did the judge tell you anything that might help me find his killer?"

"No. He was already unconscious when I arrived because of losing so much blood.'' Doc bowed his head. ''Homer was one of my best friends. You've got to find out what is behind all of this and you've got to do it quick.''

''I know.''

Doc stood up. ''I . . . oh, never mind. Just find the killer!''

Matt turned to his deputy. ''Festus, why don't you look around. Most likely, the shooter entered off the alley by the back door.''

''I saw him,'' Mildred said, stepping forward in a nightgown.

Matt could not mask his surprise; Mildred was the last person he'd expected to see in this situation. A civic leader and devoted church member, she was the epitome of propriety. ''You were here, Miss Hadley?''

''That's right.'' Mildred lifted her chin. ''Homer and I were in love and planning to get married. We slept together most nights.''

''That's none of my business.''

''I agree. But why else would I be here in the middle of the night, Marshal Dillon? And I not only saw the killer, I exchanged gunfire with him before he ran like a coward.''

''You're unhurt.''

''Yes, and that's more than I can say for Homer's murderer. I plugged him good, Marshal Dillon.''

''Are you sure?''

''Look at the carpet over there and you'll have all the evidence you need.'' She wrung her hands together. ''I have something else that might help.''

''What?''

"The intruder's gun. He dropped it when I shot him in what I believe was his hand."

Matt took the weapon, and sure enough, the six-gun was badly damaged by a bullet and its handle was sticky with blood. "I can't tell you how much this will help. Did you recognize him?"

"I'm sorry, but I did not."

"Did he say anything?"

"Not much. I think Homer recognized his voice but didn't have time to say before the shooting started."

"Ma'am," Festus said, "you were taking an awful chance!"

"What else could I do? It was either that or be killed myself. And maybe . . ."

Suddenly overcome with emotion, Mildred Hadley couldn't finish.

"Festus, keep everyone out of the yard. I don't want anyone to know we have a witness. Is that understood?"

"Sure, Matthew."

"Miss Hadley, there is no need for you to suffer a scandal."

"Thank you, Marshal, but I'm not ashamed to admit that I was in love with Homer. We were both too old to do much more than cuddle. I loved him very much."

"And I'm sure that he loved you too," Doc said. "But people can be pretty cruel and judgmental. There's no need for that, Mildred. You just stay put here until this passes and then I'll escort you home."

"You are kind, Doc. You were Homer's best friend." She sniffled. "You were also the only man that could consistently beat him at both checkers and chess, and I cannot tell you how much that galled him."

"I cheated a lot," Doc replied, looking forlorn.

"Matt, there's nothing more that I can do here."

"Then go back to bed." Matt frowned. "Miss Hadley . . ."

"Please don't allow Mr. Crump to take Homer away tonight," the woman pleaded. "I'd like to have a little more time to say good-bye."

"Sure." Matt wrapped the murder weapon in a towel, then went and inspected the bloodstains and finally the back door while Festus held off the large crowd that was already gathering out front.

It was clear that the murderer had pried open the back door to gain entrance. It was equally clear that he had not intruded into the judge's study or the second bedroom. Why wouldn't he have looted those places if he were simply a burglar? It seemed clear to Matt that the killer had come to assassinate the judge.

But why?

Matt was considering that question when he heard the angry shouting out front. He made his way swiftly outside to join Festus, who stood before a riotous mob.

"What's going on here!" Matt demanded as he planted his feet on the front porch and glared down at the large gathering.

"That's what we want to know, Marshal!"

"Is it true that Judge Blasdell was murdered!" another yelled. "Is it, Marshal!"

"I'm afraid so."

"Who did it!"

"I don't know yet."

"That's not good enough!" a different man yelled. "I think we need a new lawman, by Gawd!"

Apparently, this idea was shared by most of the mob, which shouted in agreement. Then Mr. Bodkin, the banker, pushed to the forefront. He was dressed in a bathrobe and slippers and was clearly furious. "I'm on the town council and I'm going to call a special session first thing in the morning. It *is* time for a change around here. If you can't protect us, Matt, we'll find someone who can!"

Matt tried to speak, but his voice was drowned out by the howls of the crowd.

"Matthew," Festus shouted in order to be heard. "This ain't fair!"

"It's all right, Festus."

"But it *ain't* all right! I won't work for no other marshal than you!"

"Festus, the best thing we can do is disperse this crowd and then try to find out who killed Judge Blasdell."

"Yes, sir."

They both came off the porch, shouting and waving the crowd back, but some half-drunken railroad man decided to fight. He was a big, brawny fella and he suckerpunched Matt, knocking him down. Suddenly people were all over Matt while Festus was also fighting for both their lives. Someone kicked Matt in the side of the head and he momentarily lost consciousness. Maybe he would have been killed if Festus hadn't drawn his sixgun and started shooting at the stars, forcing the crowd to scatter.

"Matthew!" Festus reached down and helped him his feet with one hand while he held off the crowd with his gun. "Matthew, you're hurt."

"Nothing that won't heal," Matt grated, drawing his own gun and wiping blood from his face before bellowing, "Everyone go home now!"

"You're finished, Dillon!" a storekeeper named Pollard called. "You're fired!"

Matt was dizzy and dazed. He stood swaying on his feet, gun clenched in his big fist. Suddenly he reached up and tore his badge from his vest.

"Matthew, what are you doing!"

"I quit!"

When the crowd heard these words, they cheered, and when Matt staggered off to clear out his office in the middle of the night, the only thing that Festus could think to do was to quit as well.

Back in the office, they shut the door to drown out the heckling mob. Festus hurried over to his boss and friend, saying, "Matthew, don't do this."

"They're going to sack me anyway tomorrow, so it makes no difference," Matt said, finding a rag and wiping blood from his face. "And besides, I'm not going anywhere until I get to the bottom of these murders."

"If you quit, I'll quit, too."

"No," Matt commanded. "They're just as likely as not to use you for my replacement."

"I'll refuse!"

"Don't do that," Matt told him. "Take my job, if it's offered. That way, at least you can help me solve these murders."

"This is wrong, Matthew. After all you did for these people for them to turn on you like this."

"They're scared, Festus. I bear them no hard feelings. We should have caught the man that murdered young Dawson and Reverend Paulson weeks ago. So far, I haven't done very well and they've a right to be upset."

"But—"

"It'll work out," Matt told his friend.

160

Festus's expression was bleak. "Matthew, I don't have any idea how to find the murderers. Do you?"

Matt didn't look up as he grabbed a pair of saddlebags and began to clear out his desk. "It had to be either Nick or that missing peddler."

"But can we prove it?"

"We have to find the man whose blood is on the murder weapon," Matt said. "He's been shot in the hand and so it shouldn't be all that difficult."

"That sounds easy, but we couldn't even find the fella that Fang chewed up."

"I know. But we'll find this one. Festus," Matt said, looking ten years older than he had the day before, "we have no choice because this won't end the killings."

"Matthew . . . I . . . I'm sorry. It's not fair that you're taking all the blame for not finding the killer. I been a-workin' on this, too."

"Keep working on it." Matt forced a weary smile. "Don't worry, I'll be close and we'll solve this thing, Festus. Mark my word."

Festus nodded and tried to speak but he felt so bad he couldn't. There was a big old lump in his throat and it ached. So he just sat down in his old office chair and watched until Matt finished stuffing his saddlebags and then silently headed out the door.

"Matt!"

He turned to see Kitty rushing across the street, then pushing through the angry crowd to take his arm. "You're hurt."

"I've been hurt before."

Kitty turned and lashed out at the crowd. "Have you all gone mad! What is the matter with you, anyway?

Matt Dillon has been your marshal and friend for too long to deserve being treated this way."

"He's out, Miss Kitty," the saddlemaker called. "Judge Blasdell has just been murdered!"

"I know," Kitty said. "But I also know that Matt and Festus are doing everything humanly possible to find out who is responsible."

"That ain't good enough. Who knows who will be next! It could even be you!"

"Never mind," Matt said. "Half of them are drunk and the other half are just scared."

"Come on over to the Long Branch," Kitty said, leading Matt away. "Until tonight, I've always thought Dodge City had its faults but I've been proud of her."

Kitty scorched the people with her hot eyes as they made their way into her saloon. She took Matt into her office and sometimes sleeping quarters and poured them both some good Irish whiskey. "Drink up."

Matt was not a big drinker but his head was throbbing and he couldn't recall when he'd felt so depressed and miserable. "Good stuff, Kitty. We ought to be drinking it for a celebration instead of my getting fired."

"Oh, I'm sure that the town council will come to their senses and realize that there isn't a man your equal to be found."

"I don't know," Matt said, "and frankly, I don't much care right now."

"You will tomorrow."

"I quit and gave my badge to Festus."

"He'll gladly give it back."

"I don't believe I want it back."

Kitty stared at him for a long while, then poured them both another drink. "Are you serious?"

"Never more so."

"Being a lawman is your life."

"Maybe it's time I found a new life."

"Such as?"

"I don't know." Matt shook his head. "I know enough about guns to be a gunsmith."

"You'd be bored to death."

"How about a . . . a freighter or a merchant of some kind?"

"No," Kitty said. "You'd hate those occupations as well."

"Kitty, I can't be a marshal forever."

"I know, but you've still got a few good years left in office. Besides, Dodge City and Festus both need you."

"And you don't?"

Kitty's eyebrows arched in question. "I didn't know we were talking about us."

"Maybe we *should* talk about us," he said. "Maybe we could get married and leave Kansas. I like Colorado and so do you."

"Not enough to move there permanently."

"Then name the place and we'll try it on for size."

"Matt?" Kitty came over and knelt by his side. "You're not talking like the Matt I know and love."

"I'm talking about getting married!" He lowered his voice and took her hands in his own, the knuckles all bruised and bloodied. "Kitty, I thought you . . ."

"What?"

"Well, you know."

"Say it, Matt."

"I thought you loved and wanted to marry me."

"Now, whatever gave you that idea?"

"Kitty, I—"

"Oh, Matt," she said, smiling. "I'm sorry. I shouldn't try to tease you at a time like this. And the truth is that I adore you and would love to marry you."

"Then let's do it."

"No," she said in a voice that brooked no objection. "Not like this. Not with you feeling as you do and these murders tearing Dodge City apart. You wouldn't like yourself very much if we just pulled up stakes and abandoned Doc, Sam, Festus, and all the rest of our friends. You couldn't live with that on your conscience."

Matt sighed. "As usual, you're right. But I'm no closer to solving these murders than I was a month ago. I know that Nick and Flora are behind them, but I can't prove it."

"Keep trying," Kitty urged. "Something will break. Sooner or later they're going to make a mistake and—"

Her urging was interrupted by a loud banging on the door. "Who is it!" Kitty shouted with unconcealed annoyance; she had left specific orders that they were not to be disturbed.

"It's Festus. Matthew, I got to talk to you right now."

"Come on in," Matt said. When Festus burst inside, his eyes were huge and he looked terrible. "What's wrong?"

"It's Hannibal. The Dawson cowboys just brought in his body. Matthew, someone gunned him down!"

Matt was out of Kitty's chair and moving across the room with the Irish whiskey still clenched, forgotten, in his fist. Festus and Kitty both rushed after him, and when they burst out of the Long Branch Saloon into the street, they saw an even bigger and angrier crowd than there had been before.

"Someone killed Hannibal!" a man shouted. "Which one of us is next?"

It took every bit of skill and effort that Matt and Festus could muster to quiet the crowd and keep them from going on a rampage, and it was nearly dawn before Hannibal's body was resting in Percy Crump's mortuary parlor.

"When is this nightmare going to end?" the mortician wailed. "I appreciate the business, but my Gawd, not this much this fast and not this way!"

"Let's arrest Nick," Matt said.

"On what charges?"

"I don't know yet," Matt replied. "But I'll think of something."

But when they got to the Red Dog Saloon, Nick was gone and Flora was drunk and defiant. "You can't arrest my boy without a reason!"

"Then I'll give you a reason," Matt said. "And it has to do with the Dawson Ranch inheritance. With Hannibal and Judge Blasdell added to the list, it all adds up to your son killing off Abe's witnesses to his last will and testament."

"What!"

"These last two murders make that clear beyond any doubt," Matt said, noting that Festus's jaw had dropped. "And it is also clear that the only two witnesses left are Austin Sinclair and Bill Varner!"

"You're mad!"

"Flora, where is Nick?"

"He ain't here."

"You're under arrest."

"For what? I ain't killed nobody but I'd sure like to kill you!" Flora cried, taking a swing at him. Matt easily blocked the punch, grabbed her long, dirty hair, and dragged her kicking and screaming toward the street.

"My son will cut your gizzard out for this!"

"Good!" Matt grated. "Tell him to hurry up and come visit, because I'm going to see that he and you *both* swing for murder."

"You've no proof of anything!" Flora screamed. "Nothing! I'll . . . I'll sue you for this!"

Matt laughed without warmth and dragged the cursing witch off to jail. Maybe her arrest would bring Nick running to her aid . . . but he doubted it.

CHAPTER

14

"Deputy Haggen, you sure better get me a drink of whiskey or I am gonna start screamin' like a panther!" Flora shouted from her jail cell.

"I can't do that," Festus stubbornly replied. "Matthew never gave whiskey to a prisoner and so I can't either."

"You idiot! Don't you understand that I *have* to have my whiskey!"

"Now Flora, I don't think you need a drink that bad."

"Look at me!"

Festus didn't really want to look at Flora but he did anyway. She was awful gray and sickly-colored, and when she stuck her hands through the jail bars, he could see they were really shaking.

"Festus, if you have a shred of mercy in your body, get me whiskey!"

"I just can't do that."

"Then I will die!"

Festus had to admit that Flora already looked like death. He was in a real quandary when Doc Adams entered and went over to help himself to a cup of coffee.

"Doc, I got to have a drink!" Flora cried.

Doc took one look at the woman and said, "I'm afraid she's telling the truth, Festus. My medical advice would be to give her a little whiskey. Otherwise, she could go into convulsions and die."

"I ain't got no whiskey in the office."

"Then you'd best go over to the Long Branch and get a bottle from Kitty," Doc suggested. "I'll stay here and watch over things. You buy the morning paper yet?"

"No, I been watchin' over Flora all night, half expectin' trouble."

"Hmm," Doc mused. "The town council is having their special meeting this morning and I'm sure they're going to have second thoughts about firing Matt. That would be pretty stupid and even they ought to be able to figure that much out."

"Matt resigned," Festus told him.

"Then he'll reconsider. The important thing is that we've got to put a stop to these murders."

"We sure do!" Festus exclaimed. "And Matthew won't rest until that's done."

"You're all a bunch of stupid fools!" Flora called from her jail cell. "The three of you put together ain't smart enough to . . ." Her voice trailed off.

"To what, Flora?" Doc asked, going over to stand before her with his coffee in his hand.

"Never you mind." Flora went back to the bunk,

where she lay down. "You just tell that fool deputy to bring me some whiskey."

"Better do it," Doc advised, noting how badly she was shaking. "I'll be fine here with this old drunk."

"Drunk!" Flora screeched. "Why, Doc, if there wasn't bars between us right now, I'd rip open your throat!"

"Doc, don't get within reach of that witch," Festus warned a moment before heading out the door.

When he was gone, Doc went over to Matt's desk and sat down to enjoy his coffee. "Well, Flora," he said in a relaxed, conversational tone of voice, "what are we going to talk about?"

"I got nothing to say to the likes of you."

"Now, that's a pity because I know that your son was wounded last night. Shot in the hand. I expect that sooner rather than later he's going to have to come to me or risk blood poisoning."

"Nick is fine."

"Oh?" Doc asked with a tolerant smile. "Flora, I very much doubt that. You've got him hiding someplace and he's hurt bad. I expect that wherever he's at is not the cleanest place in the world, and that will also help to bring on infection."

When Flora said nothing, Doc continued. "You've seen gangrene rot flesh, haven't you, Flora? It's nasty and smelly stuff. It's a shame that Nick will lose his arm."

"What are you talking about?"

"I'm telling you that without medical attention, his flesh will rot away and he'll have to have his arm amputated. If he waits too long, even that won't help."

"Shut up! Losing his arm would be better than—"

169

Flora caught herself just in time and clamped her mouth shut.

"Than what?" Doc asked. "Hanging? Well, I'm not so sure. At least when a man hangs he dies quick. But once gangrene sets in, death can be slow and extremely painful. It might take days or even a week. But it will happen."

Doc extracted a handsome briar pipe from his coat pocket and then a tobacco pouch. He packed the pipe and lit it, sending big clouds of blue smoke curling lazily into the air. "Nothing better in the morning than a couple cups of Festus's coffee and a smoke."

"I sure wish he'd hurry with that whiskey. And it better not be Miss Kitty's worst stuff."

Doc chuckled, for he was enjoying working on Flora's mind. "Miss Kitty's worst whiskey is better than your best. But I wonder if Nick is starting to feel that gangrene moving up his hand yet. I'm told it tingles and burns before turning the flesh black."

"Shut your mouth!"

"Nick didn't kill young James Dawson, the reverend, or Forbes Montgomery, did he?" Doc said, watching her face carefully. "Someone else did those murders."

"I ain't listening to you!"

"Matt and I figure it must have been one of those two men that Nick brought to Dodge City. They were his friends in prison, weren't they?"

When Flora didn't answer, Doc went on. "They fit the descriptions that Matt received and we're just waiting for their wanted posters to arrive. Once they do, we'll know for certain that it was Charlie Roe and Moses Parker. When we find one of them, they'll talk to save their hides."

"Doc, if I ever get the chance, I'll see you rot in hell."

"Not much chance of that," Doc said, emptying his cup and getting a refill. Returning to Matt's desk, he cocked back his derby, tamped his pipe with a horseshoe nail, and smiled. "Flora, we know why all these murders are taking place. You and Nick are trying to get control of the Dawson Ranch. That business last night was about finding Abe Dawson's original will."

Flora sat up, face twisted into a smirk. "Maybe he wrote *another* will, Doc. You ever think about that?"

"No."

Flora cackled. "Well, you should! Because Abe considered my Nick his son and he loved that boy."

"Don't be ridiculous."

"It's true!" Flora came over to the bars again. "One of these days you're all going to have proof of how much Abe loved my Nick."

Doc blew steam from his coffee. "None of this matters, since Nick will have died of blood poisoning by then."

"Liar!"

"I'm telling you the truth." Doc would have continued, but the front door opened and Bodkin the banker appeared. "Where's Dillon?"

"I have no idea." Doc had never liked this man and he made no attempt to hide his feelings. "Why?"

"The town council just met."

"Come to your senses, did you?"

"That's right. We fired Dillon and are sending out telegrams looking for a better man as his replacement."

Doc sat up so fast that he spilled hot coffee in his lap. He wasn't smiling anymore when he marched over to confront the banker. "I always suspected that you were a complete fool, and now you've just confirmed the fact."

"I'm not going to trade insults with you, Doc. Where is Deputy Haggen?"

"He's over at the Long Branch getting whiskey."

"What?"

"It's for Flora. She needs a drink."

"I sure do!" Flora called. "And it's going to be a toast to Dillon getting fired. Good work, mister!"

Bodkin wasn't flattered by Flora's praise. "Well, Doc," he said, ignoring the woman. "When Festus Haggen returns, you can inform him that the council has voted to install him in office as Dillon's replacement until we can find a qualified marshal. So, until then, he'll be making another twenty dollars a month and we expect him to earn his raise."

"I'll pass the news on to him," Doc promised. "But let's get back to Matt's replacement. Are you and the other members of the town council really so obtuse that you think you can hire a better man for the job?"

"What do you mean 'obtuse'?"

"I mean idiotic."

Bodkin flushed with anger and headed for the door. "We got to find out who is murdering folks around here. Doc, there's a killer loose on this town, or haven't you noticed?"

"I noticed all right."

"Tell Haggen we expect some action or he'll be the next one looking for another job."

When the man was gone, Flora burst into wild and half-hysterical gales of laughter. Doc found a towel and tried to clean the coffee stain off himself, which only made the woman laugh louder. Doc poured another cup and then he reached inside his coat pocket and produced a small, flat silver flask. Raising it to Flora, he took a drink, smacked his lips, and smiled with satisfaction.

"Want a taste, Flora?"

"Why, sure!"

He drank again. "Oops," he said, shaking the empty flask, "sorry, I just finished it off."

Flora stared at him, fuming.

Festus returned about fifteen minutes later with a bottle in his fist. "Any trouble?"

"Nope," Doc replied. "But I overestimated the town council. Festus, you've just been given Matt's job and a twenty-dollar-a-month raise."

"I don't want his job, though I could use the extra money. Who told you?"

"Bodkin."

Festus uncorked the bottle, found a cup, and poured three fingers. "Here," he said, going over to the cell and extending the cup through the bars.

Flora tossed the whiskey down. "More."

"I don't think I'd better."

"You fool! I can drink that whole bottle and you'd never know it from looking at me. Doc, tell him to pour me another cup. And this time a *full* one."

"Better do it, Festus."

Festus did so with reluctance, then frowned as Flora gulped down the second serving. "You sure can drink."

"I could put you under the table."

"I expect that's true but I ain't the one that is behind bars and bound to dance on the gallows."

"And neither am I," Flora said, scrubbing her lips with the back of her arm. "Dillon is out and you'll be next, Haggen. Then this town will hire a real marshal and deputy. Ones that don't hound the decent and law-abiding folks of Dodge just because they live on the wrong side of the railroad tracks.''

Doc snickered and prepared to leave. ''Do you know where I can find Matt?''

''He's having breakfast with Kitty at the café next to the Long Branch. I talked with him for a minute or two just now.''

''How is he?''

Festus relaxed. ''He said that he might go fishing to-day. Can you imagine? I told him that wasn't fair but he told me that he could do anything he wanted now that he was no longer in office. Doc, I ain't been fishin' all summer!''

''Don't whine to me about it,'' Doc said. ''I've in-vited you down to the river plenty of times and you always had something better to do.''

''Well,'' Festus said, ''I ain't much for fishin' any-ways, if the truth be known.''

''If Matt goes fishing, maybe I'll join him,'' Doc said, pausing with his hand on the doorknob. ''Oh, and Flora?''

She didn't reply but looked his way.

''Gangrene begins within twenty-four hours. After it gets into a man's blood and starts to poison it and the flesh, it moves real fast. I figure Nick hasn't much time left.''

''Shut up!''

Doc left chuckling to himself and deciding that it might be a good idea to go over to the telegraph office and see if anything important had arrived from his colleagues in Wichita, Newton, or Caldwell regarding a dog-bite victim.

"Sorry, Doc," the telegraph operator said. "But I do have a letter from the prison folks that Matt Dillon might be interested in seeing."

Doc couldn't contain himself and tore open the envelope. Sure enough, there were two wanted posters with good sketches of both Charlie Roe and Moses Parker.

"Is it important?"

"You bet it is," Doc replied. "And be sure and let me know if any telegrams arrive from doctors informing us of dog bites."

"I will."

Doc hurried over to the café to find Matt and Kitty seated at a window table enjoying breakfast. "Well," he said, "if you don't look like a couple of lovebirds without a care in the world."

Matt managed a thin smile. "I don't know why you think that. Kitty turned down my marriage proposal last evening."

"Aw, Matt," she said, frowning. "You know the reasons."

"Well, I don't and I'd like to hear 'em," Doc said, dragging over a chair and signaling for his usual breakfast of eggs, bacon, toast, and coffee. "Why'd she turn you down, Matt?"

"I'm unemployed."

"Not for long, I'll bet," Kitty said.

Doc pulled the wanted posters out of his pocket. "I expect you'll be glad to see these."

Matt studied them carefully. "Just like we figured. Trouble is, if I can't find this pair, I can't arrest them for murder or tie Nick and Flora into the assassinations as well.''

"Where do you think they're all hiding?" Kitty asked.

"Beats me," Matt said. "But at least now we know who we're looking for and someone might see and recognize them. I'll go over to the newspaper office. They have a fella there that will reproduce these drawings so that I can send them out to the nearby towns.''

"What if they've left Kansas?" Doc asked. "What do you do then?''

"If I get any leads, I follow and arrest them.''

"But you're not a lawman anymore," Kitty reminded him.

"No, but I am a citizen and I can make an arrest and worry about the consequences later.'' Matt looked at Doc. "How's Festus holding up this morning?''

"He's all right. Flora was going crazy for the need of a drink and I told Festus she might die if she didn't get one.''

"Would she?" Kitty asked.

"It's entirely possible. She's in very poor health. And I put a scare into her when I told her that Nick could get gangrene if he was the one wounded by Mildred Hadley last night. I gave her plenty to fret about.''

"Well, it's true, isn't it?''

"Yes, it is," Doc said.

Matt finished his breakfast. "I think I'll go over to the Red Dog Saloon and poke around while Flora is in jail. Maybe I'll find something interesting.''

"I better come along," Doc offered without much enthusiasm.

"Why?''

"Because I fully expect that you have a few enemies there and might need my services."

"You could be right," Matt decided. "And I'd welcome your company."

"You two be careful!" Kitty looked worried. "Things are bad enough around here without you both getting beat up . . . or worse."

"We'll be fine," Matt promised. "And it could be that Nick is hiding there right now. It's worth a look."

"Did you really propose marriage to her?" Doc asked as they walked up the street, crossing the tracks.

"I did and she refused. I told her we could go live in Colorado. She often talks about the beauty of the Rocky Mountains."

Doc nodded. "I've heard her."

"And when she said no to my offer of marriage, I told her we could live wherever she wanted, but that still wasn't good enough, Doc."

"She say why?"

"Yeah. Kitty told me that I wouldn't be happy doing anything but being a town marshal and that we both had too many friends here to leave behind."

"Smart woman."

"I'd have to agree," Matt said as they approached the Red Dog and noticed a couple of rough-looking cowboys lounging on the front porch giving them hard stares. "Doc, maybe you coming along wasn't such a great idea after all."

"I'm sticking with you."

"Okay, but are you packing a gun?"

"No. I'm a physician. Remember?"

"What good is a physician without his medical kit?"

Doc merely grunted as he followed Matt past the two

scowling cowboys into the Red Dog Saloon. There weren't many customers at this early hour and the usual bartender had been replaced by a huge man with bulging biceps.

"What do you want?" he demanded.

"I'm looking for Nick," Matt told him without preamble.

"Too bad. You're out of a job, Dillon, so take Doc and get out of here while you still can."

Matt placed both hands on the bar. "Mister, are you threatening me?" he asked in a quiet voice.

The giant nodded and rolled his massive shoulders. "Dillon, you got no badge to protect you anymore. You're just a has-been that is out of line. So git!"

"Matt?" Doc whispered as several of the other customers rose out of their seats and stood glaring at them. "Maybe we should reconsider."

"Why don't you do that, Doc?"

"I meant we *both* leave!"

The giant grinned, showing missing teeth. "You'd better listen to Doc. Either that, or get ready to pay for his services."

"I think I'll look for Nick," Matt said, starting around the bar toward the supply room and Flora's office.

The giant rushed forward to block his path. He and Matt were about the same height, but Flora's bodyguard was the heavier, stronger man. Matt tried to step around him, and when the giant grabbed his arm, Doc saw Matt stomp his boot heel down on the giant's foot hard enough to crush the bartender's toes.

"Owww!"

Matt drove an elbow into the big man's solar plexus, doubling him over, and then he whipped a left hook to the giant's jaw that sent him crashing to the floor. When the man attempted to get up, Matt kicked him in the gut. He shrieked.

Matt whirled around to face the other customers, gun suddenly appearing in his fist. "You boys have had enough to drink," he said. "Get out of here while you can."

There was a stampede for the door, and when the saloon was empty, Matt handed his six-gun to Doc, saying, "If this one tries to get up, shoot him in the knee."

"All right," Doc breathed.

Matt disappeared for about fifteen minutes. Doc heard him crashing around in Flora's office and the stockroom, then he heard the angry protests of Flora's girls as they were rousted out of their cribs. When Matt returned, he glanced behind the bar at the big man, who was still moaning.

"Nothing of the other two?" Doc asked.

"No," Matt answered. "But we'll find them no matter how long it takes."

Doc dipped his chin in agreement and returned Matt's gun. He looked down at the giant and shook his head, saying, "Bed rest. You need to go to bed and don't move for a couple of days."

The giant didn't seem to hear him and kept moaning. Doc figured that there was nothing more he could do or say to help, so he followed Matt out of the Red Dog Saloon.

CHAPTER

15

After putting Charlie out of his misery, Moses Parker had thought long and hard about whether or not to return to Dodge City. If he did so, he would face the wrath of Flora and Nick, which was not a trifling matter. Also, he was not sure how they would react when they learned that he had been forced to shoot Charlie. Moses supposed that he could lie about it and say Charlie had lost his nerve and run off, but that would be a difficult sell since Charlie had been a very greedy man. And where else would someone that ugly ever make a big pile of money?

There was also the matter of Marshal Dillon and Deputy Haggen. They had seen him in the Red Dog and had been looking for him with some hard questions to ask. Moses didn't fear anyone but he knew better than to tangle with a lawman.

The arguments for returning to Dodge City were simple and had everything to do with money. More money than Moses could hardly imagine, if they gained control of the Dawson Ranch. A spread like that would be worth a fortune and Moses figured he was due a piece of the action.

So, he could ride away and play it safe . . . or he could run the risks and hope luck was finally in his corner. All his life he'd been waiting and watching for the opportunity to become rich and he figured this was as good a chance as he'd ever have again.

Moses chose to return to Dodge. But not in the peddler's wagon. No, sir! He would grow a beard and ride in on horseback late at night. He'd pay a visit to Nick and Flora and tell them straight up why he'd had to kill Charlie. Maybe they'd even be happy. After all, there would be one less piece of the pie to split if everything worked out just right. And they probably needed his gun and rifle to kill a few more of the witnesses. *Yes,* Moses thought, *they'll welcome me with open arms and probably congratulate me for killing poor old Charlie.*

So he spent a week in Newton and a few more days in Caldwell, where he sold the peddler's wagon and one of the horses for a tidy sum of money. Then, when he'd grown a beard and felt like he was at least halfway disguised, he saddled up and headed for Dodge, arriving late at night and going directly to the Red Dog Saloon.

"Where's Flora?" he asked the bouncer with the big arms.

"Where have you been?"

"I been gone. Why?"

"Maybe you ain't heard. Flora is in jail and Nick is on the run."

Moses blinked. "What happened?"

The man told him, and when he'd finished his story, Moses said, "So Nick killed both Hannibal and Judge Blasdell?"

"Whoa. I didn't say that. I told you that they were murdered and that Dillon got sacked and his deputy is takin' his place."

"Do they really think that Flora killed them two witnesses?"

"I don't know. But she's in jail and you can hear her screechin' like a wildcat every morning. She ain't gettin' enough whiskey, you know."

"Yeah," Moses said, "and I'll bet she's making Festus's life miserable."

"She and Nick needed you," the giant said accusingly. "They needed you and Charlie to do some jobs."

"Charlie isn't going to do any more 'jobs,' " Moses replied. "He's dead."

"Dog bites killed him?"

Moses patted his six-gun like the shoulder of an old friend, grinned coldly, and said, "Bites and one of my bullets."

It was the giant's turn to gape with surprise and fear. Moses was pleased. "Whiskey," he ordered. "A bottle of the good stuff."

"Comin' right up!"

Moses carried the bottle to an empty table. It was about midnight and he was dog-tired and now totally unsure of what was going to happen next. Maybe the smartest thing was just to climb back on his horse, ride out of Dodge City, and never look back. But what would he ride to except a bunch of nothing? And he hadn't hardly been paid by Flora for the killings he'd done so far.

Moses knew that he just couldn't swallow that much disappointment. What to do then? Only one thing came to mind and that was to visit old Flora, so he scooped up the whiskey bottle and headed for the back door.

"Hey! You comin' back?" the giant yelled.

"Probably."

Moses found an empty whiskey keg and he toted it around behind the jail. He had to stand on his toes to peer through the bars but he could sure hear Flora snoring. Moses wondered if Haggen was sleeping in the office, but he doubted it. Most often, the lawmen locked up everything and went home until morning.

"Flora!" he hissed. "Flora, it's me, Moses! Wake up!"

The snoring continued. Moses wasn't sure what to do, but since it sounded like Flora was asleep directly under the barred window, he poured her a little whiskey on her. The results were instantaneous. Flora not only stopped snoring, she sputtered and cursed.

"Shhhh! It's Moses. We need to talk."

A moment later her ghostly and ruined face appeared in the pale moonlight. Flora's hair was tangled and she was a mess. Moses leaned back a little when he caught a whiff of her breath. It was so fetid it could have killed flies.

"Where you been, you ungrateful cuss!"

"I had to take Charlie off because he was in a fever."

"Where is he?"

"Planted beside the Arkansas River. Don't worry, he'll never be found."

There was a long silence, then Flora whispered, "Good! My boy is hiding alongside that river, too. You need to help him get away."

"Why—"

"He was shot in the hand and grazed across his forearm. Doc Adams tells me he's going to get gangrene. You ever seen the black rot?"

"I have. It's . . . it's real bad."

Flora sniffled. "The flesh rots and goes black. You got to put Nick in that peddler's wagon and take him off to a doctor!"

"I sold the wagon."

"What! You fool!"

Moses didn't much appreciate being called names and had killed more than one man for that indiscretion. But he bit back an angry retort and said, "I can steal another wagon or an extra horse. Tell me where to find Nick and I'll help him get off somewhere."

"You ain't gonna kill him like you did Charlie, are you? If you did that, I swear that I'd kill you slow. And if I couldn't do it, I got enough money to pay men who could."

"Don't threaten me, old woman. Just tell me where to find Nick and I'll have him twenty miles from here by morning."

"You better take him to a good doctor. I'm scared for Nick. He's all I got left to live for in this awful world."

There was a trace of desperation and pleading now in the old woman's voice that Moses hadn't thought possible. "Yeah, I'll take him to a doctor."

"Moses, you'd best remember that my boy is the only one that can get you a piece of the Dawson Ranch."

"I know that. Stop worrying. I won't kill him."

Flora didn't seem to be listening. "If this works out,

I'll see that you are a rich man. You'll never have to kill anyone again."

"Sure. Now, where is he?"

Flora told him and ended by asking, "Did you bring me whiskey?"

"Yeah. Here."

The old woman's hand snaked through the bars like the talons of a turkey buzzard and she practically tore the bottle from his grip. A moment later, Flora slid back down into darkness and Moses could hear the soft gurgle of whiskey draining down her ugly gullet.

He got his horse and found another saddle horse tied in front of the Lucky Dice Saloon. It was a tall, dark gelding that looked as if it could run fast and far. Then Moses rode back out into the night down to the river. Flora's directions weren't too good, however, and he didn't find Nick and his cave until shortly after dawn.

"Nick! It's Moses! Don't shoot."

"Moses, where you been?"

"Nick, it's a long story and we're out of time, so come on out and let's ride before people are up and about. We got to put some miles between us and Dodge City in one hell of a big hurry."

Nick crawled out of the cave already looking half-dead. He was so filthy and thin that Moses hardly recognized his old prison friend. "Damn, Nick, you don't look too good."

"Help me into the saddle," Nick ordered. "And tie me down tight. Where we going to hide now?"

"We'll find a place."

"No more caves," Nick muttered. "No more!"

"All right. Somewhere else. Maybe a farm. Yeah.

We'll find a little homestead to hole up in until things get better.''

That seemed to satisfy Nick and they rode east as fast as their horses would run and Nick's strength would allow.

It was a hard three-day ride from Dodge City to the doctor in Wichita and Moses didn't think that Nick was going to last. His color was gray, and by the time they finally arrived at the rail town and a very upset Dr. Lathrop took him under his care, he was as feverish as Charlie had been.

"Why in the devil did you wait so long to bring this man in to me!" Lathrop demanded after Nick collapsed in his waiting room. "Don't you know that he might very well die!"

"I did the best that I could," Moses said. "So maybe you better quit jawin' and start doctorin'."

"It may already be too late. I might have to amputate at the elbow."

Moses shook his head emphatically. "I know Nick and he'd rather be dead than one-armed. Just treat him as best you can."

"Who shot him in the hand?"

"Don't matter, Doc. Just treat him and do it now!"

Lathrop was young and strong enough to have likely whipped Moses for being so threatening, but something in the stranger's eyes made him take a step back and then stammer, "Sure. I'll . . . I'll do what I can for your friend."

"I figured you would. Doc, I'll be back tomorrow either to pay for his buryin' or for your work."

"All right."

Moses found a hotel room, a bottle, a juicy red steak, and then a red-haired woman in exactly that order. He also got drunk and slept until noon. When he awakened, he discovered that the woman had robbed him. Angry, and with his head pounding something awful, Moses went back to the saloon, yanked his six-gun, and pointed it at the bartender.

"What's wrong!" the man exclaimed, looking down the pistol barrel.

"She works here and her name is Dora. She has red hair and a mole on her right cheek the size of a pill bug. You tell her to bring back my money this afternoon or I'll hunt her down and kill her. Understood?"

"Yeah, but why you pointing that gun at me!"

" 'Cause I feel mean enough to kill you, too."

Moses turned on his heel and left the saloon. He had six bits hiding deep in his pocket and that bought him the breakfast he needed. After four or five cups of coffee, he was feeling better and returned to the saloon.

"Here is your money, mister," the bartender said, holding it out with a hand that shook. "No hard feelings."

Moses counted it down to the last red cent. "No hard feelings," he answered when he was satisfied all but three dollars could be accounted for and he'd probably spent that much on liquor.

Afterward he went to the mercantile and bought himself a new shirt, hat, and two pairs of stiff blue Levi's. They felt good and the hat sported a high peak that made him look much taller. When he arrived at the doctor's office, the news was good.

"Your friend is going to live."

"With his arm, right?"

"Yes. But I had to amputate two fingers."

"The little one that was black and the one next to it?"

"That's right."

"Okay. How much do I owe you?"

"Five dollars."

Moses paid Dr. Lathrop. "Nick ready to ride?"

"No! And he won't be for at least a month. He's very weak and unwell."

"We ain't got that long, Doc. I'll take him now."

"I think you ought to at least give him another day or two under my care."

"So you can charge me another five dollars. No thanks."

Nick was heavily sedated and had to be practically carried to the hotel. Moses laid him down on the floor and covered him with a blanket, then he lay down on the bed and went to sleep. He decided that he would give Nick four or five days in Wichita. After that, they'd head back toward Dodge and he'd try to figure out their next move. Maybe they could find a farmhouse to hole up in for a while until Nick got stronger. Yeah, Moses thought, that would be a good idea.

The homestead was about twenty miles east of Dodge City, nestled up in some rolling hills. There wasn't much except a few weathered outbuildings and Moses could see that the original homesteaders had built a soddie. It was still being used for storage but the owners had erected a small frame shack that didn't look half as solid as the soddie. Moses could see a couple of corrals with horses and a cow. There were also a few pigs lounging around near a little stand of trees fed by a well that ran

189

sparkling down past the sorry shack. This was certainly not a prosperous homestead, but it would sure do.

"Hello the house!" Moses called as he rode into the yard and reined in his horse among a flock of noisy chickens.

"Hello there," a woman answered from behind her curtains, so that he could only see her silhouette. "Who are you and what do you want?"

"I got a sick man here. Like to pay you for some supper and to sleep in that there soddie. Looks like a storm comin' in and my friend already has a fever."

"Doc Adams can be found in Dodge. Ride on, stranger!"

Moses shook his head. "I'm afraid my friend won't stand up to another twenty miles, ma'am. Maybe I should speak to your husband."

"He's . . . he's gone off to gather our cows. Be back real soon, though. You go on, now."

Moses removed his hat and studied the shack. He didn't see any sign of children and the place was real run-down. Maybe this woman was alone.

"Ma'am," he said, dismounting and leading his and Nick's horses over to the well spring. "We've got to rest now. So we'll just take our rest in that there soddie and wait to speak to your man when he comes back."

There was a long silence. "I . . . I think you should ride on to the next place. It's only a couple miles west. They got better eats. Maybe they'll feed you supper."

"This is just fine. I'll kill us one of these hens and roast her up fine. Pay you a dollar for her, too!" Moses grinned. "A dollar is a lot more'n a chicken is worth and these hens are real skinny."

"I got a rifle on you. Show me the dollar!"

He showed her. "See?"

"Drop it where you stand and don't you bother me nor my family no more. And don't burn down the inside of our soddie, neither!"

"Yes, ma'am. But it'd be hard to burn one down seein' as they're all dirt."

"With rafters in the ceiling!"

"Yes, ma'am." Moses helped Nick out of the saddle and led him into the soddie. "You lie still and rest."

"What's the matter with that woman?" Nick whispered.

"She's scared . . . and she ought to be."

"Don't hurt her," Nick said.

"Just don't you worry about me or that woman. Worry about yourself."

Nick went outside. He could still see the dim silhouette of the woman and he was all-fired curious to know if she was alone and if she really did have a rifle in her hands. And how old was she? She sounded kind of young. Maybe she was even pretty.

Moses strode out into the yard and surveyed the chickens. He picked what looked like the fattest of the hens, drew his gun, and shot its head off without even aiming. The sound of his gunfire fled like a frightened ghost across the lonely hills.

"I'm awful good with a gun or a rifle," he bragged, grinning toward the shack. "You a good shot, ma'am?"

"I am. Don't test me."

"Now, why would I ever do such a thing!" Moses holstered his gun and enjoyed watching the headless chicken flopping crazily around the yard. "I'm a generous man. Just paid you a dollar for that there chicken and we both know she ain't worth but maybe two bits."

"She was a good layer, mister, so you'll get no thanks from me."

"I could use a few potatoes and some salt. Pay you another . . . nickel."

"No. Just stay away from this cabin or I'll kill you."

"Why you hiding in there like a spook or somethin'?"

"I got a sickness."

His grin soured. "What kind of sickness?"

"A fever. You come near me you'll likely get it."

"Has your husband got the fever?"

"He has not! He's well and he can shoot straight, too."

"Well," Moses said, "I look forward to meeting him. If he has any whiskey to sell, you tell him to come out tonight and join me for a friendly drink."

"He don't drink the devil's brew."

"Yes, ma'am."

"Go take care of your sick friend and leave me alone to my own misery."

"I'll just do that," Moses told her. "Yes, ma'am, I surely will."

He found some old branches and made a good fire. He wasn't much for plucking a chicken cold but he was hungry and a dollar was a lot to pay, so he cut it up, roasted it on a stick, and took but half, giving the rest to Nick.

"Wish we had some salt and something good to go with this tough chicken," Nick complained.

"Me, too." Moses was sitting in the doorway, eyes fixed to the shack. "Maybe after a little while I'll go see if she has something more."

"She said she had the fever. You leave her alone."

"Sure," Moses said, not meaning it. He would sleep a few hours, then creep over to the shack and try to get inside. Maybe it was crazy and she did have the fever and he'd get it and die or also fall ill. But curiosity was a powerful thing and he just had to find out what this woman looked like. He was sure by now that she had no husband chasing cattle.

He thought that she probably had no husband at all.

CHAPTER

16

Margaret Ellen Cobb was afraid that she was going to recover from whatever fever had killed her husband and her two children, one by blessed one. She didn't know why she had survived, but she did know that it wasn't fair, that being dead was better than being alive when you'd lost your whole family. The fever had been given to them by a sick family passing through a few weeks earlier. Margaret should have known better than to take them into her house and try to help them recover. They'd continued on their journey after two days but left their sickness behind. First to sicken and die was five-year-old Becky Ann, then her brother, James. After that, her husband had wilted with grief and just seemed to give up and die of the disease and maybe also a broken heart.

One by one they'd each been buried in the good dark soil that had once been their little vegetable garden. After Albert was gone, Margaret had not had the will or the strength to do anything, and by then, she had also fallen victim to the deadly disease that had destroyed her family. She'd prayed for a quick death, and when that hadn't come, she tried to put a gun to herself and end it all . . . but couldn't because her father had been a Baptist and her mother a devout Catholic. Both had instilled in their only daughter the belief that a person would go to eternal damnation and hell if they took their own life. And so, Margaret lived only for the time when she would die and then might hope to be reunited with her family in heaven. She'd put the gun away and survived weeks of misery until she began to recover.

It wasn't fair! Why, she railed at God, couldn't she be reunited in heaven with her beloved family? How come!

And now this intrusion. Two men invading her misery and now resting out in the soddie, defiling it more than the chickens and the livestock. One man sick and the other a no-good gunfighter, judging from his looks and words. What was she to do if the gunfighter came to pay her a visit tonight? Could she kill him? Margaret wasn't sure but she thought she might. Or he might kill her and then her soul would not be stained by the act of suicide.

Yes! If he came to try to force himself on her in the darkness, she would fight and make him kill her and then this horror would be past.

The more Margaret considered this possible escape from a living hell, the more she became convinced that it might be a blessing in disguise. And if she were forced to kill the gunfighter, wouldn't that be justice? Thou shalt not kill was a commandment but Margaret was sure that God would not judge her too harshly if she took a life in self-defense.

She fed her fire and brushed her hair that evening, often gazing out her window toward the soddie and sometimes seeing the man looking right back at her. Margaret was certain he was evil. Maybe he was waiting to kill the husband she no longer had or he was building up his nerve and his desire to defile her already ravished body.

She cleaned Albert's gun and laid it on the wooden table he had sawed and built and where she had fed her family these past seven years. She also had a shotgun and made certain it was loaded and close to the bed. And, for insurance, she slipped a butcher knife into the pocket of her dress. When the evil man came, she would pull out the knife and slash him and then he would take the knife away and kill her in his rage. Yes, Margaret thought, that was the way it would be.

Margaret wondered if the gunfighter had killed women before. Some men would kill men but not women. What if this was such a person? Well, he couldn't be, that's all. She would cut his face. He had a good face and was probably vain. Cut his face and he would lose his mind in such a rage that he would kill her for certain.

The hour grew late and her last candle waned and flickered. The moon floated through the lace of her window curtain and Margaret expended much of her remaining strength pacing the good wood floor that had cost her and Albert so much but had also given them such pride. She had torn up a section of the floorboards to make crude coffins. Margaret could use a hammer and nails just as well as most men, since Albert had taught her and he had been a handy and resourceful man.

Come on, she thought. *I know that you are thinking of me like a wolf might think of a helpless lamb. Like a hawk might a tender dove. Come into my house and I will cut your grinning face and maybe your throat so that you will kill me and then perhaps die yourself.*

Come on, and give me the death that I was cheated out of and now so much desire!

As if he could read her mind, Moses Parker left the soddie and she heard the whisper of wood and leather hinges as he pushed her door open and stood silhouetted in moonlight and dying candlelight.

"Your husband is gone or he would have returned long before now," Moses said with laughter in his voice. "You're alone and you have no man."

She tried to keep a tremor from her voice. "I have a husband and I believe I will see him very soon."

"No, you won't. And you ain't sick anymore." He took a step inside and Margaret saw that he held his gun loosely at his side. "Woman, what really happened?"

She could not lie and saw no reason to try. "My husband died of sickness and so did my two children."

"I don't believe it. I see no sign of children."

"I buried everything with them."

"You're well," he said, holstering his gun. "And I think you are still young and pretty . . . but awful thin."

"I am diseased. You . . ." Margaret forced herself to say the words so that God would remember that she had not lied or truly deceived this grinning Lucifer. "You should go away. Take your sick friend and leave while you can."

"I'll leave him out there and sleep with you."

"No."

198

He came up to stand before her. "You ain't so bad. And I ain't so bad either. Maybe we can help each other."

"For the last time, go away!"

He reached for her left hand and she went for the butcher knife with her right. His face was only inches away when she brought the sharp blade up and slashed his throat. Blood poured out over both of them and he made a strangling sound as he tried to claw for his six-gun.

Margaret fell back and watched as he dragged the gun up, aimed it at her, and attempted to fire, but he staggered and then the gun slipped from his wet fingers and he lunged forward, one of his hands clenched to his throat and the other locking on her throat.

Kill me, too! Don't die before you crush my throat or throttle me just as your own life ebbs and flows upon Albert's wooden floor.

Margaret wanted to close her eyes and pray for death but she could not tear her gaze from his face as it contorted in helpless rage. She was only faintly aware that he was trying so very hard to kill her and she thought that he might succeed since she could not breathe. A crimson veil dropped over her eyes and she matched his death grin as she spiraled into absolute darkness.

Margaret Cobb awoke the next morning with sunlight shafting through the doorway to warm her face. For several happy moments she believed she was standing in the light of God's presence but then a cloud passed across the face of the sun and she realized she was still alive. Her thin body convulsed and tears welled up and ran down her sunken cheeks. She lapsed into something that was not sleep but was certainly not wakefulness.

Rather, it was a nightmare that did not end until she again opened her eyes and realized that it was raining very hard and that the wind was howling and tearing at her curtains and lace.

Margaret rolled to her hands and knees and then she saw the dead man and remembered with shocking clarity what she had done and what he had *not* done.

She scrambled to the doorway and stared across the yard, which the rain had already turned into a quagmire. The chickens were roosting in the henhouse and her corralled horses were facing away from the wind, tails plastered wetly between their haunches. The soddie stood open and staring at her and Margaret now also remembered that there was another devil inside and that he was sick.

But what if he was not so evil as the one whose throat she had cut? Whose life she had taken in direct contradiction to the laws of God? What if he were . . . a good man whose life she could save. Would that not somewhat atone for the life she had taken last night? And then would God allow her the mercy of death?

Margaret did not know, but her mind seized on this as a possibility. And so she pushed herself to her feet and staggered out across the yard, pelted by the cold, driving rain, until she stumbled into the soddie and saw the man lying sick on a soggy blanket with his eyes staring at her blacker and deader than yesterday's oven coals.

"What is your name and were you sent here by Satan?"

"What?" His voice was a dry, cracking whisper.

"Are you also a devil!"

"No," he wheezed, and then lapsed into a terrible fit

of coughing. "I am a sick man. Please help me!"

Margaret wavered.

"What happened to Moses!" he choked as another bolt of lightning split the sky and the earth shook with the shock of rolling thunder.

"I killed him. And maybe . . ." She had to say it. "I will also kill you!"

"Then don't just talk about it," he said, teeth rattling like a box full of little bones. "Go ahead and kill me!"

It was then that she knew he did not belong to Lucifer, because no true devil would ever want to be killed . . . for any reason.

Margaret looked up at the rain and then she went and took his hand. "We have to get back to the house where it is dry and I can start a fire. Can you walk?"

"No."

"Then we'll crawl."

"I can't!"

"Then you'll die of your own choice," she told him as she started to turn and leave.

"Wait!" Nick begged. "I . . . I will try."

She was disappointed. "Come on, then."

He was terribly weak. Even weaker than herself. But he was determined and pulled himself outside. Lightning speared across the stormy sky and Margaret smelled sulfur or smoke. She grabbed his wrist and tried to drag him through the mud.

"Come on!"

"I'm trying."

And he was, so she helped and, somehow, they reached the cabin.

"Holy . . ." His words died and he stared at Moses lying in a dark stain of his own life's blood.

201

Margaret ignored the dead man and got a fire started. She was shivering violently and huddled close to the warmth, the man crabbing over to join her.

"You cut Moses's throat!"

"And I'll cut yours as well if you try to touch me."

"I wouldn't," he said. "You ain't even pretty."

She had once been very pretty but didn't feel the need to tell him so. In fact, now that her husband and children were gone, she wanted to be ugly and as gray as the world.

Slowly, the shack grew warm. He looked around until his eyes came to rest on the hole in the floor. "What happened?"

"Coffins for my family."

"You killed them, too!" His eyes grew round with fear and his heart began to race.

"Disease killed 'em. I only killed your friend."

"Oh." Nick swallowed hard and the hammering in his ears quieted. "I been shot in the hand. I been feverish."

He waited for a sympathetic reply from the woman but received a dull silence, so he finally added, "I have money and can pay you for food. Do you have anything to eat?"

She tore her eyes from the flames and stared at him so long that he thought her mind must surely be addled. "I have."

"Would you cook something for me?"

"Why?"

"I'm awful hungry, ma'am."

She seemed to consider this from all angles and then she got up and went to a sack in the corner, removing potatoes along with beans and two ears of horse corn.

She found a black-bottomed pot, then some water from outside, and put everything on the stove to heat. Soon he could smell the food and he was so famished he drooled.

"Suppose you could help me to the table and maybe wash this mud off me so I could eat?"

She did, using a stiff, dirty rag.

"My name is . . . George," he lied. "What's yours?"

"Mrs. Cobb."

"No, your first name."

"Mrs. Margaret Ellen Cobb."

"I'm sorry about your family dyin' of sickness."

She turned to stare right though him. "Why?"

"Because I . . . well, I am. And don't you feel too bad about Moses. He was a pure killer and you did the world a big favor. Did he die quick . . . or slow?"

"You talk too much, mister." She got up from her chair and forked the corn and potatoes onto a tin plate, then added beans. "Eat and be still."

He inhaled the food . . . every last morsel, leaving her nothing. Burping noisily, he looked over at her dry bed. "I need the warmth of blankets and sleep."

She forced herself up and laid blankets on the floor. Nick could tell by looking at her face that he had better not ask for anything else.

When he awoke again in the night, the woman was gone and the door stood wide open to the prairie wind. Nick could see a million glittering stars and knew that the storm had passed. Moses was gone, too, a long dark bloodstain across the floor his only legacy.

She is crazy, he thought. *And she might try to kill me next if I do not kill her first.*

Nick felt strengthened by the food and this new resolve. He crawled around in the semidarkness until he found a shotgun. It was loaded and he would kill that crazy loon when she returned and then he would have whatever food was left in this charnel house.

CHAPTER

17

"**M**arshal Haggen?"

Festus looked up from his newspaper and frowned with annoyance. He didn't much care for Barney the telegrapher nor did especially appreciate being called "marshal" instead of "deputy," which he considered himself to be despite the raise and temporary promotion.

"What is it?"

"I got something you're gonna be real interested in seein'."

Festus laid his paper down and then dropped his boots to the floor. Since Matthew's resignation, nothing had changed. He still had the small desk and the worst chair and that was just fine. He'd also neatly stacked Matthew's mail on his desk. To Festus's way of thinking, it was only a matter of time before Matthew returned to his rightful position as marshal of Dodge City, Kansas.

"What is it?"

"A telegram from a Dr. Lathrop in Wichita. He says that he treated a man with his finger shot off and then happened to hear about the man that Mildred Hadley shot after he broke into Judge Blasdell's house a while back."

Festus jumped out of his chair and rushed across the room to snatch the telegram out of Barney's hand. The message was short and contained no more information than he'd just heard from the telegrapher.

"You gonna go to Wichita and try to catch that fella? Could be he's the same one that also robbed and killed Mr. Montgomery."

"Could be," Festus said, thinking the exact same thing.

"If you was to be the one that caught the killer, might be they'd make you the *permanent* marshal of Dodge City."

"I don't want to be the 'permanent marshal,' " Festus answered.

"Big pay raise and you might finally be able to find a woman who'd marry you."

"Barney, why don't you keep this news under your hat?"

"Why?"

"Well, dad blast it," Festus fumed, "ain't there some sort of oath or somethin' that you fellas are supposed to take, promisin' that you'll not blab everything you read that comes over the wires?"

"Festus, that's a real poor way to treat a fella that just did you a mighty big favor. I figured you'd be grateful instead of threatening."

"I am grateful," Festus assured the man. "But I still wish you'd keep quiet about this."

"What are you gonna do, Marshal?"

"And stop calling me 'marshal'! Matthew is still this town's real marshal."

"Well, I got to say that you're the only one that thinks that way. And since you're being paid as a marshal, you ought to start actin' like one. Are you goin' to Wichita after this fella that Doc Lathrop treated?"

"I don't rightly know yet."

"Festus, it could make your career in Dodge City!"

"Thanks, Barney. Now, if you don't mind, I got work to do."

"What work? Readin' the newspaper?"

Festus bristled. "I got to keep up on stuff in this here town, now, don't I? Now git!"

The telegraph operator was disgusted and made an uncomplimentary sound as he passed back outside, but Festus really didn't care. The minute he was out of sight, Festus hurried over to the Long Branch Saloon, where he found Matt and Kitty.

"What's all the excitement about?" Kitty asked. "You look like you just inherited a fortune."

"Maybe better than that, even." Festus handed the telegraph to Matthew, who read it in a glance and then came to his feet.

"Festus, you could be right," he said. "Maybe this is the break that we've both been waiting for."

"You goin' to Wichita?"

"I sure am," Matt replied, dragging out his pocket watch. "The next train leaves in one hour and I will be on it for sure."

"Can I come with you?" Festus asked expectantly.

"I'm afraid not," Matt told him with a shake of his head. "You're the marshal now and in charge of keeping the peace."

Festus just grumbled.

"Matt," Kitty said, "maybe I should go with you."

"I can do this better alone . . . but thanks for the offer."

Matt wasted no time in preparing for his short train trip east. He knew the marshal of Wichita, whose name was Race Tucker. Tucker was a good man and would certainly assist him in making the arrest if the killer was still recovering in his town. And so, when he boarded the train and headed for Wichita, Matt could not help but feel optimistic. He'd check in with Marshal Tucker as a professional courtesy, then find and interview Dr. Lathrop. With any luck, he might have the killer by nightfall and he'd bet anything that it was either Nick Dawson or Moses Parker.

When he arrived at Tucker's office late that afternoon, the marshal was just locking up his office and heading home for supper with his pretty wife and two young sons.

"Matt! What are you doing here?" Tucker asked.

"I came on business."

"I heard about the town council firing you and couldn't believe they could be so stupid. Anything I can do to help?"

"Just tell me where I can find Dr. Lathrop."

"Why?"

In a few words, Matt told the marshal of Wichita about the telegram that he'd received and the implications it presented. "If I can find the man that Lathrop treated, I'm betting I've got the same one that killed

208

Forbes Montgomery and several others in my town."

"I'll take you to see Lathrop."

Dr. Lathrop was also about to close up his practice for the day but he was eager to help catch a murderer and said, "I knew right away that it was a bullet wound. I had to amputate two of his fingers."

"Would you give me a description of the man?"

"There were actually two of them. The one that was shot was the larger. Dark features and rather handsome. Maybe six feet tall but thin and in rough shape. I also noticed he was real dirty. Filthy, actually."

"That would be Nick," Matt said. "What about the man that brought Nick in for treatment?"

"Also pleasant looking, but shorter with brown hair. He was ordinary looking and seemed pretty nervous. Can't blame him, I guess. I wanted the one that I treated to stay at my place so that I could guard against any further infection, but the other one insisted that they leave. I think they went over to the Buckeye Hotel and stayed."

"Did they come back for any more treatments?"

"No, but they should have. The infection was a long way from being cured and the man had a high fever."

"Have you seen either of those men since?" Marshal Tucker asked.

"I'm afraid not. Do you think that they were the ones that are responsible for all those Dodge City murders?"

"I'm almost certain of it," Matt answered. "And Doc, if they should return, I'd be grateful if you'd let Marshal Tucker know immediately."

"I'll be happy to." Lathrop frowned. "I heard that you were fired, Marshal Dillon. I'm sorry. You have quite a fine reputation . . . one even I've heard of."

"Thanks," Matt replied. "Especially for the telegram. It might be just the break we've been hoping for since all this trouble began."

"What is behind this rash of Dodge City murders?" Tucker asked.

"Money. Lots of money."

"A bank job?"

"No," Matt answered, "a huge inheritance that certain people hope to gain by killing off everyone and anyone who might stand in their way."

"Sounds very interesting."

"It is if you consider murder to be interesting. Race, I've got to find these two men that the good doctor has just told us about."

"Then let's go over to the Buckeye Hotel and ask questions. Someone is bound to know something."

"What about your family?" Matt asked. "You've probably got supper on the table."

"It often has to wait," the marshal replied. "Clara knows that my job sometimes comes first. In fact, it usually does. And besides, I just want to get you started. With luck, we can find out when those two killers left and where they went. Maybe they're even still right here in my town!"

"I doubt that," Matt responded. "It would be too easy and nothing about this has been easy so far."

"It almost never is," Race Tucker agreed as they thanked Dr. Lathrop and hurried over to the Buckeye Hotel.

The proprietor was out but his clerk was able to identify the two men as Moses and Nick, or at least Matt was pretty sure they were from his description.

"They stayed to themselves. The shorter one went out

sometimes and brought back food for the sick one. I never seen the one with the bandage on his hand but once when they checked in.''

''How many nights?''

''Six or seven.''

''When did they leave?'' Matt asked.

The clerk opened his register, ran his finger down a column of names, and clucked his tongue. ''They've been gone three days.''

''I don't suppose they said where they were going?''

''Afraid not,'' the clerk replied. ''Sorry.''

''Thanks for your help,'' Matt said, feeling let down as they strolled outside.

''What now?'' Tucker asked.

''I'm not sure. They could have gotten on the train and headed east.''

''We can go down to the ticket agent and see if he remembers them.''

''All right,'' Matt said. ''Let's do that.''

But the ticket agent did not recall such a pair. ''I'd remember a man that was shot in the hand,'' he assured the two marshals. ''They never boarded my train.''

''Then they had to leave by horseback,'' Matt reasoned out loud. ''The question is, where did they go?''

''Wish I could help you,'' Tucker said, looking equally disappointed by this setback. ''What do you think?''

''I'm not sure,'' Matt said. ''But, if I were in their shoes, I'd be looking for a safe place to hole up and hide.''

''I could start checking all the saloons and hotels this evening,'' Tucker suggested with an obvious lack of enthusiasm. ''I'd be happy to do that for you, Matt.''

"No thanks. I can do that myself. You go home to the family. The truth of the matter is that I'm almost certain that they've left."

"But where'd they go?"

"I don't know," Matt admitted, "but you can be certain that I'm going to put some thought to the matter in the next few hours while I snoop around here asking questions."

Matt didn't find out much more information about Nick and Moses. At the Lone Star Saloon, he met a bartender named Fred who well remembered Moses Parker. "We got a gal named Dora and she robbed him. He came here and pulled a gun on me and, Marshal, I never seen such cold eyes in my life. He'd have shot me dead if I hadn't promised to help get his money back. And I did, you can be sure of that."

"Maybe I had better talk to Dora."

"She left town. Maybe went to Caldwell. I don't know. She was just a restless, thievin' tramp that almost got me shot."

"Thanks," Matt said. "I don't suppose that you saw what color horses they were riding?"

"Bays. Both of them tall bay horses. I saw 'em ride out three, maybe four days ago."

"Going which direction?"

"West. But they might just have been going to the general store or blacksmith shop or some other place in town and then headed off in another direction: So don't take my word they rode west."

"I just about have to," Matt said. "And besides, it makes sense."

"I hope you get that one fella that threatened to blow my head off. He didn't look like much out of the ordinary until he shucked his gun and pointed it right here between my eyes." The bartender placed his forefinger on the spot. "And when he did that and I looked into *his* eyes, I knew he was a killer and he'd shoot me dead with no more thought about it than you or I would give to swattin' a fly on the wall."

"I'll try to get him," Matt said.

"If'n I was you," the bartender called as Matt turned away heading for the door, "I'd shoot first and ask questions later. He was real fast with that hawg-leg. Real fast!"

Matt interviewed several other people and a few of them remembered Moses and Nick. Especially Nick, because he'd been so weak and ill. A bullwhacker was able to confirm that the two men rode bay horses west out of town and that the taller man was bent over in his saddle and looked mighty weak and pale.

Matt didn't take the train back to Dodge City. Instead, he rented a livery horse and outfitted himself with three days' worth of food and gear. Enough to scour all the vast rangeland between Wichita and Dodge City. Especially the places where a couple of savvy fugitives like Moses and Nick would choose to lay low.

He figured that a man like Moses would be looking for a farmhouse or homesteader's shack to hide. And since he'd want to keep in touch with Flora Dawson, the closer to Dodge City the better. Given that reasoning, Matt didn't waste his time heading north or south but basically followed the railroad line west, where he was most likely to see a homestead off a ways to the north, generally easy to find because of planted trees.

He got a late start and darkness found him on the prairie, so he hobbled his horse and spread his bedroll on the grass. Not wanting to bother gathering cow or old buffalo chips for a campfire, he ate a cold supper of crackers and tinned sardines washed down with water. The moon had melted to a quarter its whole and the stars were bright and blinking.

Matt had always enjoyed camping out on the range in good weather. He'd done it many times and was comfortable with the solitude and the night. It seemed that he could look up at the moon and stars and they gave his mind inspiration for good thoughts and ideas. Tonight, he thought about Kitty and how, for the first time in the longest time, he was unemployed and not carrying a badge. It wasn't so bad. Actually, if Kitty had accepted his offer of marriage, he reckoned he could have put being a lawman behind . . . that is, once he had Nick and this Moses Parker safely behind bars.

I'd be a good gunsmith, he thought, *and I think I'd like it well enough. But maybe I'd get bored with fixing guns after a while. Well, then I'd just have to think of something else to do for a living. I know I wouldn't enjoy owning a saloon like Kitty. Too many headaches and I'm the kind that likes to go to bed early and get up at daybreak. Also, I don't enjoy the drunks that come with that trade and have to be dealt with in a friendly fashion. Maybe I could run a livery. Naw, I wouldn't enjoy cleaning stalls and feeding stock. Then . . .*

Matt fell asleep thinking about what he could do if he didn't get his job back as the marshal of Dodge City. In the end he figured maybe he would just buy and sell horses or invest in a business. He had savings. Nearly three thousand dollars, and while that was not nearly enough for him to retire on permanently, it would give him the time and the resources to explore other lines of employment and business.

He awoke at first light just as always and grained his livery horse. It was a good animal and he'd promised to turn it in at the freight yard in Dodge, where a man would tie it to the back of a wagon and return the animal on his weekly freight run. Matt sure missed his morning coffee but he was in a hurry, so he saddled the horse and rode on with the sun already starting to warm his back.

That morning, he stopped at two homesteads but neither family had seen anyone resembling the pair he sought. At the third homestead, however, he heard some interesting news from a man named Cletus Adams. "You might want to ride off a ways north and check to see if Mrs. Cobb has seen anyone passing her way. She's recently a widow who lost her husband and two children of the sickness."

"She lives alone out here?"

"Yeah," Adams said, "she refuses to go into town. If you ask me, I think the loss of her family addled her mind. She'll run off anyone that she thinks is trying to take her place away. I don't know how she'll survive this winter. I think she'll freeze or starve out. Maybe you can talk some sense into her, Marshal."

"Well, Mr. Adams, I'm not a marshal anymore," Matt confessed. "But I will speak to the woman and see what can be done. There are people in Dodge who are kind and would take her into their homes if she's willing to work for her keep."

"Oh, she's a hard worker, all right. But real odd."

"Point me in the right direction," Matt said.

"You mean you can't stay for dinner?" Adams was

a tall, skinny man with two tall, gangly sons and a short, thin wife with prematurely gray hair. "My boys can chop the head off a chicken and then Mabel can boil it up tasty."

"I'd like to stay and eat with you," Matt said, knowing by the looks of things that killing a chicken would amount to a sacrifice for these good people who barely seemed to have enough food to keep themselves. "But I have to ride on. Here's a dollar for your time and information."

The man stared at the silver dollar. "Well, I . . . I can't take that."

"Why not?"

"Didn't do nothing for to earn it!"

"Oh, yes you did," Matt argued. "If you hadn't told me about the Cobb homestead, I would have missed it for sure. And anyway, it's official money I'm given to pay for information. If you don't take it, I'll have to write up some report telling the town council why not. So you'd be doing me a big favor by taking the dollar."

"Well, okay," Adams allowed, snatching it from Matt's hand. "Doesn't seem right, though. But I don't want to put you to extra work."

"I'm much obliged," Matt told the homesteader, nodding to his sons and reining his horse off in the direction of the Cobb place. He twisted around in his saddle. "How many miles?"

"About ten."

Matt nodded and put his horse into an easy lope. He'd be there in less than two hours.

CHAPTER

18

Margaret Ellen Cobb had left the shack and gone out to the corral to saddle one of the devil's horses. With no food or water, she'd mounted the tall bay in her ragged skirts and set off with no particular destination in mind. She had decided to ride until daybreak and then turn the horse free. After that, she would lie down in the grass and stay down until she was dead. Margaret wasn't sure if that was the same as committing suicide and thus breaking God's law. She wasn't sure at all. But she could not go on living and so she was prepared for whatever consequences awaited her at heaven's pearly gates.

What she did know was that the devils had come and defiled her homestead. Before, her family's place had been only diseased, now it was also unclean and unholy. It was a place of death and murder and she wished to be away from it as soon as possible.

When dawn arrived, Margaret dismounted in a low place between two big grass-covered hills and then un-saddled and unbridled the horse. "You are free to roam," she told the tall gelding. "And if you are wise, you will run north, where the land is still open and the wind runs free and clear."

But the bay took off toward Dodge City, tail up, mane flying in the breeze. Margaret watched until the animal was just a dark dot on the landscape, then she lay down on the cool grass and prepared to die, wondering just how long it would take. She was very weak, so she thought it might only take a day . . . possibly two. No more, certainly. She supposed that thirst would be her only real trial; her stomach was shrunken and she had long since conquered the pangs of hunger.

Placing her hands on her chest, she closed her eyes and began to pray. "Our Father who art in heaven . . ."

Matthew didn't know why he happened to be riding over the top of a hill and looking down to see the woman lying so small and still. This land was so vast that the chances of seeing her down in the low place seemed more remote than finding a needle in a haystack. And yet there she was, with her yellow hair and her faded dress.

"Oh no," he whispered, galloping down the hill and pulling his mount up a few yards off. The horse rolled its eyeballs at the still figure and then its nostrils flared and it snorted in fear, indicating to Matt that the woman was probably dead. Or maybe it was because the animal smelled the dark, crusted bloodstains on the front of her faded dress.

"Easy," he said to the animal, which was wanting to bolt and run away. "Easy."

Matt calmed his horse and led it forward until he could kneel by the woman's side, and then he grabbed her wrist and felt for a pulse. At first, he thought there was none but his eyes argued that there must be, for the woman's bosom was rising and falling. Matt bent closer and placed his ear to her nostrils and felt the warmth of her faint breath.

"Ma'am? Ma'am!" he called, shaking her hard.

Margaret stirred and then she moaned. Her eyelids fluttered then stopped and Matt could see that her face was badly burned by the sun and the wind. He soaked his handkerchief with his canteen and gently patted cool water on her badly cracked lips, then her eyes and face. "Ma'am! Wake up!"

This time Margaret's eyes did open, but they seemed unable to focus and her bloody lips trembled. Suddenly she shivered and screamed.

Matt reared back and stared into the woman's eyes, sure that she was insane. "Easy," he whispered. "I mean you no harm. Are you wounded? What is your name?"

The lips pulled back from teeth and she hissed, "Devil!"

"I'm no devi!. Are you Mrs. Margaret Cobb?"

She did not answer but he saw something change in her expression, so he said, "I'm thinking you are Mrs. Cobb. Here, try to take a drink out of my canteen."

She shook her head. Matt was afraid that she carried a killing disease that could well claim him along with her husband and children. But he couldn't leave this woman and so he slipped an arm under her and lifted.

Margaret weighed little more than a half-grown child, but she struggled against him for a moment and then fainted.

I've got to get her to Doc Adams. Got to forget about finding Moses and Nick and try to save her.

Matt's horse gave him fits and he had a tough time trying to hoist the unconscious woman into his saddle and then climb up behind. Twice, the animal shied and almost dumped the half-dead woman. But at last he managed the job and then he held her tight and put the spurs to his mount. Matt wasn't certain, but he reckoned he was about twenty miles northwest of Dodge City.

It occurred to him that he might be bringing sickness and death to Dodge. The more he considered the possibility, the more worried he became. Finally, when he spotted the big stockyards to the north of town, he rode hard toward them. Two cowboys galloped out to meet him and Matt shouted, "Stay back! This woman may be sick. Go find Doc Adams and tell him to come out and help!"

The cowboys had only to look at Margaret Cobb to see that she was, indeed, diseased and near death. They reversed direction and headed for Dodge at a hard run. Matt rode over to the stockyard and dismounted. He laid the woman down in the shade of a corral fence and tied his horse to wait.

Doc Adams arrived about a half hour later on foot. He was flushed and out of breath. He was also out of sorts. "Doggonit, Matt, why didn't you bring her into town?"

"It's like I told those two cowboys, she's diseased."

"Hmmph!" Doc snorted. "She looks dead."

"She isn't."

Doc knelt at her side and lifted Margaret's eyelids, asking, "How do you know she has a disease?"

"A neighbor told me she lost her husband and two children to some affliction. Doc, I didn't feel I could take the chance of bringing her into town."

"You thought right," Doc said, feeling for her pulse. "We're going to quarantine the three of us for a couple of days while we sort this thing out."

"Quarantine?"

"You heard me right. We're going to stay away from everyone else until we know what we are dealing with here."

"Doc, I've got to ride back out and find Nick and Moses."

"Not until we see if you come down with whatever killed this poor woman's family."

"But—"

"I'm sorry. Nick and Moses will keep."

"But they won't! Their trail could run cold."

"You've no choice." Doc leaned close. "Do you really want to risk the chance of spreading an epidemic and killing innocent folks?"

"No." Matt swore in helpless anger. "How long will we have to be quarantined, Doc?"

"I don't know. If this woman survives and I can find out some particulars and identify the cause of her family's death, maybe not too long. But if not or she dies, we need to give this thing at least a week."

"A week!"

"That's right. Now, let's stop moaning and arguing and see if we can figure out someplace to take care of her that is better than this but that won't be in anyone's way or danger."

"There's an old work shack at the other end of these stockyards."

"Then help me carry her over there and let's try to save her life."

"I don't expect you can, Doc."

"Well," he grumped, "I just might surprise you!"

Once in the shack, Doc Adams went to work while Matt shouted to some cowboys to send Festus out to see him. The new marshal arrived in record time and would have run up and pumped his hand, but Matt shouted, "Stay back! Diseased woman, here!"

Festus retreated. "You got something bad, Matthew?"

"We don't know. Doc says it will take a few days to see."

"What about the woman?"

"She might die."

"What . . . what are we gonna do now?"

"Wait," he replied. "We'll just have to wait for a few days and see how this shakes out."

"Any luck in Wichita?"

"Yes. It was Nick and Moses Parker, all right. Moses had a couple of fingers amputated."

"What's that woman got all over the front of her dress?" Festus asked.

"Dried bloodstains."

Festus gulped. "Her own?"

"No," Matt answered. "Someone else's."

"Matthew, I sure wish you weren't in this fix."

"Me, too. How is it going in town, Marshal?"

"Aw, Matthew, you're the *real* marshal. You know that I didn't want this job. I want to be just an ordinary deputy again. Now I got everyone growlin' and fussin' at me so bad that I can't even leave the jail and go have a drink or a meal in peace. The only good thing is that the judge let Flora out because we had no evidence to keep her, so at least I don't have to listen to that wailin' all day long."

"Just do your best and this will pass. I'm not real happy about being stuck here for days while Nick and Moses might be putting distance between us."

"He might not be wantin' to leave his ma and run off someplace far."

Matt nodded. "I've thought of that. Dr. Lathrop in Wichita said that Nick was in real bad shape when they left town. I'm wondering if they didn't find Mrs. Cobb here and drive her off her own homestead."

"They'd have killed her, Matthew. We both know they would have."

"I suppose so."

"You want me to go out and find her place and take a look-see?" Festus said eagerly.

"Let me think about it. If something went wrong in Dodge City and I am stuck here and you were out of town, who'd handle the trouble?"

"I dunno and . . . well, Matthew, right now I don't much care. I know that sounds plumb awful but I sure am sick and tired of this marshalin' business!!"

"I'm afraid that you're going to be stuck with it awhile longer. I'm not even sure if I'll ever be reinstated."

"Be what?"

"Be asked to put my badge back on," Matt explained.

"If you don't, I'm quittin'!!"

"You can't, Festus. At least, you can't for now."

"Dang it!"

Matt turned and peered back into the little work shack. He could see Doc trying to force water down Mrs. Cobb's throat and then he heard her gagging and coughing. "Festus, you'd better go back to town and wait."

Festus looked bleak as he reined his horse around, saying, "I'll make sure you all got bedding, food, and drink."

"Thanks. Just keep the townspeople away."

"Once they hear that this woman is dyin', that will be easy. Matthew, if anything were to happen to you or Doc, well, I'd . . ."

Festus couldn't find the words, so he spurred his horse off and galloped back to town.

The curiosity seekers in Dodge City all came out that next week to sit on the grass and stare at the shack where Doc, Matt, and Mrs. Cobb were quarantined. On Sunday, some of them even brought baskets of food and spent a few hours picnicking on the open range. Matt didn't like it, but there was no help for it, so he ground his teeth and held his silence. The only good part was that it appeared that Mrs. Cobb would survive. That had seemed an impossibility to him when he'd first spotted her down in the draw, but now she was sitting up and talking to Doc and her color was much improved. True to his word, Festus had kept them well stocked and the weather held fair, so they didn't even have to huddle in the little work shack in order to keep dry.

"Now that you're feeling a little better, I have a few questions to ask you, Mrs. Cobb. That is your name, isn't it?" Matt asked.

"Yes, sir."

"I heard about your family all dying off and I want

to say how sorry I am. How sorry we all are. But what I need to talk about is where you got those bloodstains all over the front of your dress. Mind telling me?''

"They were both devils," she said, eyes looking north. "I had to kill the shorter one when he tried to take me down on the floor and do the devil's dirty work. The sick one was going to kill or defile me, too, so I ran away."

"The sick man's name was Nick and I understand from the doctor in Wichita that he had two missing fingers on his right hand . . . the little one and the one next to it."

"That's right. He was real weak but still mean through and through."

Matt frowned. "So you just ran away?"

"That's right. I was all fixed up to die on the prairie when you appeared and messed things up real good."

"You're too young to die."

She shook her head. "Mister, I am far, far older than my years and I already seen enough misery and sorrow to last two lifetimes. Nothing left for me to live for now that my kids and husband are dead."

Doc was puffing on his pipe, staring out at the northern range, but now he turned and studied the scarecrow woman thoughtfully. "I could use an assistant, Mrs. Cobb. You know anything about medicine or nursing?"

"I know plenty."

"Well, we could give it a try. I'd pay you cash along with room and board. Of course," Doc added, "this offer is good only if we survive."

The woman seemed puzzled and at last said, "Doc, I never worked for nobody but myself before."

"That's good, because if you had, you'd realize what

a hard man I am to be around all day. However, if you can put up with me, you can put up with anybody, and I do need the help.''

''Might be that I'll do it,'' Margaret said. ''For a little while.''

''Good!'' Doc had to relight his pipe. ''We'll stay here another two days just to make sure it is safe for the townspeople, then we'll go into Dodge and find you a place to stay.''

''I won't tolerate drunkenness or any tomfoolery. I'm a God-fearin' woman.''

''I know that, Mrs. Cobb.''

''Why would you hire me?''

''I just think you'd be a good worker and I need someone reliable.''

The woman nodded and Matt thought that this would be a fine arrangement. ''Doc,'' he said, ''it's going to take me a full day to return to discover if Nick is still holed up at her homestead. And then most of another day to get back here. I'd like to break the quarantine and go find the Cobb homestead now.''

Doc gave the matter some thought. ''All right,'' he finally decided. ''But if you come across anyone, wave them off. Go straight to Mrs. Cobb's homestead and then come straight back here to see how we are doing.''

''All right.''

Matt was never so glad to leave a place in his whole life. He saddled his horse and galloped off after Mrs. Cobb asked him to bring back a daguerreotype of her family that was resting on a bedside table.

It was late in the afternoon when he finally saw the Cobb shack and soddie. Matt dismounted and removed his rifle from its saddle boot then advanced slowly, searching for any sign of habitation. But the horses were all gone and the shack seemed empty. He rushed it at sundown but he needn't have bothered. Nick had vanished.

Matt stayed at the cabin overnight, and early the next morning he went out to the graves. Three of them had wooden cross markers but the fourth did not. In fact, the fourth grave was set so far apart from the others that it would soon be invisible. It was at this fresh grave that Matt took an old shovel and began to dig. He didn't have to dig very deep to find the already decaying body of Moses Parker. When he saw how the killer's throat had been slit, he shivered, despite his inner toughness gained over many years of seeing murder victims.

"I guess you finally tried to compromise the wrong woman," he said to the gray-faced corpse.

Matt covered the body and rode circles around the homestead until he found the tracks. One was older, one newer. Both led northwest, to where Matt had no idea, for there was nothing in that direction until you got into Colorado. Mindful that he was breaking his promise to Doc but that he had to get on Nick's trail before it disappeared, he followed the two sets of tracks heading northwest.

CHAPTER

19

O n the very first day that Matt and the mystery
woman had returned and holed up just outside
Dodge City, Flora had sent one of her customers out to
gather some much-needed information.

"Find out who the woman is and where she came
from. Find out what's wrong with her and any other
damn thing that you can," were Flora's exact orders.

Several hours later the man returned to say, "Dillon
brought back a homesteader woman named Mrs. Cobb.
She's diseased and that's why they're stayin' out there
in that little old shack."

"Never heard of her," Flora said with disappointment.

"Well, Festus is tellin' everybody that she killed
Moses."

"What!"

"That's right. Slit his throat. And there was another

man, too. They think it was Nick. Marshal Haggen was tellin' a crowd that it's Nick and Moses that is responsible for all the murders.''

''But no sign of my boy?'' Flora's heart was pounding so hard that she could scarcely get her breath.

''Nope.''

She gave the man ten dollars and a bottle of her best whiskey along with a warning. ''Don't you tell anybody what you told me. Understand?''

''Sure thing, Flora.''

''Good! Just get drunk and keep your trap shut about what I sent you out to find.''

''I'll do it. I swear!''

Flora went over to her giant bartender, whose name was Cody. ''You want to make some real money?'' she asked.

''What have you got in mind?''

''Nick is probably recovering out at that sick woman's homestead. Ask around for directions to her place without being obvious, then buy a horse and provisions and get there fast.''

''To do what?''

''Get my boy out of this territory! Take him to Denver and find a man named Alex Hawk. He's got a saloon about like this one and he owes me some big favors. Have him take care of Nick and send me a wire saying . . . saying the young dog came home.''

The giant frowned with perplexity. ''The what?''

''That'll mean he's got Nick safe.''

''Then what will I do?''

''Come back here to Dodge City.''

''What about Dillon? Festus says he's going out there

to find Nick as soon as the quarantine is lifted. Might be a week, though.''

''Perfect,'' Flora replied, uncorking a bottle and taking a pull. ''That'll give you and Nick plenty enough head start to reach Denver. If Matt Dillon follows, get my boy safe to Hawk, then kill Dillon and collect a hundred dollars from me when you bring back a piece of his hide!''

Cody grinned hugely. ''I sure will enjoy collectin' that money. Damned if I won't!''

''Then be on your way,'' Flora snapped. ''And don't you even think about waitin' to ambush Dillon until you deliver my boy to Alex Hawk.''

''You must trust this Hawk fella plenty.''

''I do,'' Flora said. ''I was married to him. He never was true to me but then I wasn't true to him neither. Mostly, though, I know he'll take care of my Nick, because he's also Nick's real pa.''

''Flora, you never told me that before.''

''I never even told Nick. But it's time he found out. Let Hawk tell him, though. And then you just see if you can bring me back a piece of Dillon's hide!''

Flora gave Cody all the money he'd need to buy provisions and sent him on his way. She knew how much he'd been festering since Matt had whipped him so bad. Cody would kill Dillon and he would kill him slow.

Flora cackled. ''Bet he brings back Dillon's ears, by Gawd!''

But when Cody reached the sick woman's homestead, Nick was already gone. Cody followed his tracks, pleased that they were heading for Colorado. Maybe Nick had a few of his own friends in Denver. No matter, the tracks were pretty fresh and Haggen had said that

Nick was most likely in bad shape. Cody figured he'd overtake Flora's boy and they'd ride the rest of the trail together.

Two full days passed, however, and he had still not overtaken Nick. He was growing angry and maybe that's why he didn't see that he was riding into an ambush.

Nick had seen the big man on his trail far back and figured it was Marshal Dillon. It had to be because of the man's enormous size. And so, when the rider entered rifle range, Nick took careful aim and squeezed off a shot. For a split second nothing happened, and then the big man grabbed his shoulder and tumbled out of his saddle. His horse galloped off and he lay still on the grass.

"Got him!" Nick exclaimed, coming to his feet and remounting before he continued on toward Colorado.

Cody didn't know how long he'd lost consciousness, but when he awoke, he felt weak and a little dazed. His left shoulder was broken but the wound did not appear to be fatal and the slug had passed out the back side through his shoulder blade, clean as anything. Now he had to stop the bleeding and catch up to his horse.

Stopping the bleeding proved to be the easier of the tasks. Flora's giant bartender and bouncer plugged up the hole and looked around for his saddle horse or the man who'd ambushed him. It had been Nick, Cody was dead certain about that. But why? The answer came to him as he staggered off to retrieve his horse. Nick must have figured he was Matt Dillon and close on his trail. Sure, what other explanation? Damned fool kid!

Cody's mammoth-size horse was spooked by the scent of fresh blood, as horses and most other stock most generally are. It took him four precious hours and a lot of his dwindling strength to finally grab the animal and haul himself into the saddle. Cody was mighty tempted to ride back and get his shoulder fixed but Flora would skin him alive, and besides, he wanted that hundred dollars' reward for killing Marshal Dillon. So he gritted his teeth and followed the kid's trail, hoping to overtake him in the night.

"Nick, wake up!"

Nick sat up fast, clawing for the gun lying beside his bedroll. But Cody's massive hand slapped his face and set bells to ringing. "Damn you, kid, you shot me instead of Dillon this afternoon!"

"I shot you?"

"Yeah, and I need some help."

"I ain't in real good shape myself."

"There's supplies in my saddlebags. Cook us up some bacon and beans. I'm near starved to death and weak as a kitty cat."

"Sure, Cody." Nick shook his head to clear away the cobwebs. "I'm sorry about that mistake. What are you doin' out here followin' me, anyways?"

"Your ma sent me to take you to a fella named Alex Hawk in Denver. Where was you headin'?"

"I didn't rightly know," Nick admitted. "I just wanted to get as far away from Dodge City as I could. I figure to get better, then come back and kill Dillon."

"That makes two of us. But I promised I'd take you to Hawk's place to hide out."

"Who is this Hawk fella?"

Cody almost told the kid it was his pa but he kept his vow to Flora and said, "Just a real old friend of your ma's. She said he owes her plenty of big favors."

233

"Sounds good to me."

"Dillon may be following us pretty quick, if he ain't already," Cody muttered.

"Then we'll have the chance to kill him sooner rather than later," Nick replied.

"I'm going to cut off his ears and take them to your ma as a prize. She'll probably wear 'em around her neck."

Although Nick was sick and hurting, the remark still caused them to chuckle with mirth.

"Let's eat and sleep, then get an early start," Cody said. "I'm worn down to nothin'."

"Maybe you'll feel better tomorrow."

"No, I won't," Cody replied, "thanks to you, kid. You need to know for sure who you're shootin'! You nearly killed me!"

"Like I said, I'm real sorry."

"Tell that to my poor shoulder," Cody growled. "Now get us some food to cookin' so we can eat and get to sleep."

"How far to Denver?"

Cody thought about it for a moment, then grunted, "Long way, given the sorry shape we're both in."

"We'll make it," Nick vowed. "And I hear that Denver is a real good town."

"It is."

"But after we mend awhile, I'm returning to claim the Dawson Ranch."

"Sure, kid."

"I will!"

"Get the bacon and beans and start us a cookin' fire," Cody ordered as he lay down on the kid's bedroll, holding a bloody bandage tight against his massive shoulder. "Wake me up when it's time to eat."

"Sure," Nick said, thinking about claiming the Dawson Ranch and killing Matt Dillon, but not in that order.

The tracks that Matt had followed away from the Cobb homestead turned sharply north at the junction of the Arkansas River and Big Sandy Creek. He was in Colorado now and the country was higher but still mostly flat to rolling hills. Here and there he saw a homestead, but mostly it was still wide-open plains. Matt figured that someday it would all be turned to the plow, if ranchers didn't lay claim to it first.

At a bend in the river, he came upon five men camping in a big stand of trees and called out, "Hello the camp!"

They were just sitting down to supper with a black kettle hanging over their campfire but one of them got up and came over to greet Matt.

"Stranger, where you headed?"

"Toward Denver."

"We just come from there," the man said. "We be headed for Dodge City or maybe Wichita. You from there?"

"I know both towns," Matt said, sizing up the bunch as drifters probably looking for work in the booming cattle towns.

He knew he'd judged them correctly when the man said, "There work for good men in Kansas?"

"There is. Especially if you have a trade."

"We're just a bunch of broke cowboys that have done about everything to get by," the man said, introducing himself as Slade, then asking, "What be your name, stranger?"

"Matt," he said, knowing better than to tell them that he was a lawman, or at least had been until very recently. Matt never revealed his true identity in these kinds of situations; you never knew who might have a grudge against you or maybe even just lawmen in general.

"Well, Matt, come have supper with us. It's humble but you're welcome."

"Much obliged," he said, dismounting and leading his horse over to a tree some fifty feet away from the other animals. He unbridled his horse and haltered it, tying a lead rope to an overhead branch so the animal wouldn't get tangled. Then he unsaddled and laid out his bedroll before moving over to join the others at their campfire.

"This here is Matt from Kansas," Slade said, introducing him to the other four drifters. "He says there is work to be had in them railhead towns."

"There was work in Denver, too," one dirty young man said with a slow grin, "but we ain't all that inclined to work, are we?"

They all laughed and Matt was given a plate of food. It wasn't good, but it was hot and filling and he was grateful.

"What did you do in Kansas?" one of the men asked. "You don't look like no cowboy or freighter to me."

"Oh," Matt hedged, "I done this and that."

" 'This and that'?" The man shook his head. "Sounds about like me and my friends here. We was mining up in the mountains around Central City but didn't have no luck last summer, and it's so high and cold there a man feels weak and out of breath most of the time. So we went down to try our luck at Cripple Creek but all the good claims had already been worked. When winter come along, we moved down to Pueblo and found enough work to keep from starvin'."

"Maybe you'll have better luck in Kansas," Matt told them.

"We sure hope so," Slade said, studying Matt closely. "You been in Dodge City a long time, have you, mister?"

"Awhile."

"I heard they got a real tough lawman there by the name of Dillon. You ever heard of him?"

"I have."

"Well?"

"It's a good town for people who respect the law," Matt said, cleaning off the mix of beans and stew with his forefinger and then rising to his feet. "Boys, I've come a long way and I got to leave early, so I guess I'll turn in now. I sure thank you for your company and your stew."

"Think nothin' of it," Slade said. "What are you going to Denver for?"

"Oh, just to see a man." Matt smiled, dipped his chin, and headed off to his horse and his bedroll.

"Good morning, Marshal Dillon," Slade said, prodding him awake at first light. "I'm afraid we've got some real bad news."

Matt started to reach for his pistol but then saw it had been removed. "What is going on here?"

"I reckon you've forgot the name Eddie Porter. But Ed ain't forgot you."

"Who is Eddie Porter?"

"That's me," another man said, favoring Matt with a toothy smile. Porter tipped his hat back to reveal a puckered scar leading out of his hairline. "Marshal Dillon, don't you even remember giving me this souvenir?"

"No."

"Well, you did about five years back. Sure, I was drunk and raisin' Cain, but I didn't deserve to be pistol-whipped the way you did me."

Matt remembered now. Eddie Porter had beaten a woman half to death in a drunken rage and threatened to kill any lawman who tried to arrest and jail him in Dodge City.

"What's the matter?" Slade asked. "Cat got your tongue?"

Matt knew he was in deep trouble but tried to bluff it out. "All right, I was the marshal of Dodge City, but I'm not anymore."

"That don't make my head feel any better."

"It's true that I've had to pistol-whip a lot of men when words and reason failed. I've never once killed anyone but admit that I have given a few like yourself a scar or two as a reminder to act civil."

"Oh, this was a reminder all right," Porter said, fingering the scar. "I've been reminded of it every time I look in a mirror. I'd been robbed by one of your girls and was trying to get my money back when you busted me across the skull. Wasn't fair, Matt Dillon!"

"Maybe not, but you survived."

"Well," Porter spat, face turning ugly with rage, "I'm giving you the same medicine you gave me. Boys?"

Before Matt could tear free of his bedroll, they all landed on him and then Porter pistol-whipped him not once, but three times. Matt felt the warm blood coursing down his face, and when he tried to speak, his voice was as thick as cold molasses.

"You'll pay for this!" he choked.

"We'll take our chances, Marshal."

"What are we going to do with him now?" one of the men asked.

"We ought to kill him," another said, "or it's gonna come back on us someday."

"No killing," Eddie Porter told them. "I just wanted the marshal of Dodge City to know how it feels and to have his own scar as a fair reminder that bustin' heads is wrong."

"We better take his outfit or he might come up on us tonight."

"Horse thievin' is a hanging offense," Slade informed his partners. "So we'll leave him his clothes, a bridle, and his horse, but not a damn thing else."

"I sure admire his gun and saddlebags."

"I have a hankerin' to try on his boots."

Matt shook his head, trying to stay conscious as wave after wave of pain ricocheted around in his aching skull. "You boys are in enough—"

He never finished his words because Porter struck him one last time.

When Matt finally awakened, it was nearly sundown and his head was pounding like a Comanche's war drum. He had to crawl over to a cottonwood to pull himself to his stockinged feet and he clung to the tree a good five minutes attempting to clear his head. At least they'd left him his horse and a bridle as promised. Nothing else, though. Not even a saddle.

"Damnation," Matt muttered, staggering over to the animal. He was so weak and dizzy that he was forced to use a fallen tree to mount and then he struggled to decide which way to ride—after the six men who'd done him wrong, or continue toward Denver and Nick.

Matt chose to follow Nick because he was the one behind all the killings in Dodge City. Slade, Eddie Porter, and the other misfits and drifters could wait for another day of reckoning. They were probably not murderers.

He rode for a good part of the night, but it was such a trial that a few hours before sundown he slipped over his bareback mount, tied the reins to his wrist, and fell asleep on the open prairie. When he awakened, it was high noon and his head still hurt something awful, but at least his vision was clear. He remounted and rode on through the afternoon until he saw a homesteader's cabin, where he turned in, looking for food and shelter.

"Hello the house!"

A short, stocky man emerged holding a rifle. Matt could see his wife and a girl of about five years old huddled in the doorway. "What do you want, stranger!"

"I've been beaten and robbed," Matt replied. "I need help."

The man advanced and saw the dried blood on Matt's face and the way his eyes had been blackened from the terrible beating. "Climb off that horse and we'll see what we can do," he said, lowering his rifle.

Matt got off the horse. But after that, he hardly remembered anything until the next morning, when the homesteader's wife and daughter brought him a breakfast of hominy grits, corn, and fresh goat's milk.

"I sure am obliged to you folks," Matt told them.

"And when I get back to Dodge City, I'll find a way to send you money in repayment."

"No need," the man replied. "My name is Will Blake. This here is Martha Ann and my girl, Bessie Sue."

"Matt Dillon of Dodge City."

"What happened?"

Matt told them about his being a marshal for many years and how he'd occasionally found it necessary to pistol-whip a dangerous man rather than to shoot him, especially if he was a mean and angry drunk.

"That Porter fella sure got back at you in spades," Martha Ann said. "I think you had better stay with us for a few days until you recover."

"I'd like to," Matt answered, "but I can't. I'm on the trail of a murderer. Maybe two of them. I have to ride."

"You're not up to it today," the woman told him in a way that brooked no argument. "It's more than thirty miles to the next settlement, and what do you suppose would happen if you fell off that buckskin and couldn't catch him up again?"

"I—"

"You'd likely die," the woman said pointedly. "We're Christian people and we would not be doin' right if we allowed you to leave before you were able."

"Okay," Matt agreed, knowing she was right. "I'll stay one more day and I sure do thank you for your kind hospitality."

Matt stayed the extra day and was mighty glad that he did, for he felt almost human when he rode off on the old saddle that he was loaned by the family and also a cap-and-ball Navy Colt in good working condition with spare ammunition.

"I'll drop everything off here on the way back," he promised.

"I know that you will, Mr. Dillon," the homesteader replied. "We're not at all worried except for your welfare."

"Much obliged," Matt said.

They stood before their humble little house on the prairie and waved him good-bye. It was good to meet good people, Matt thought. Especially after all the bad.

Four days later he rode into the thriving town of Denver with his eyes still blackened and puffy. Matt didn't know anyone in town, and being broke and friendless, he went directly to the marshal's office and introduced himself to the marshal and his competent-looking deputies.

"Dillon, I've heard a lot about you and all of it good," the marshal of Denver said. "I'm sorry that you had such a rough time getting here. We'll fix you up with whatever you need and help you in any way that we can."

Matt decided to tell them that he had been fired as marshal.

Marshal Joe Mingus replied, "I understand. Our jobs demand long hours at low pay and they are dangerous. Added to that is that we never receive loyalty from town councils, who can hire and fire us in the blink of an eye. But all that aside, it doesn't matter, Dillon, because your reputation is known far and wide and speaks very well for itself. Don't you worry about a thing. And if we get your man and you rest up and stay awhile in Denver, why, I'll hire you on as a new deputy."

"Thanks," Matt said, nearly overwhelmed with gratitude. "I can't tell you how much I appreciate your cooperation."

"No problem."

Mingus looked to his men and then motioned them to gather around Matt. "All right," he said, "tell us what we need to help you find this Nick Dawson fella and whoever he's ridin' the outlaw trail with in Denver."

Matt accepted a cup of coffee and related the whole bloody story, starting with the suspicious death of old Abraham Dawson and then the ambush of his son and the preacher, followed by the murders of Forbes Montgomery and Hannibal. Mingus and his deputies were silent for nearly an hour, but when the murderous tale was finished, the marshal of Denver said, "Boys, let's start askin' and lookin' for a man missing two fingers from his right hand. If you come across him, come get us first and watch out for his sidekick! We're dealin' with some bad characters here that wouldn't hesitate to ventilate your gizzards, given the opportunity."

Matt watched as all four deputies filed out the door. They were tough, competent lawmen and he felt sure that his luck had finally turned from bad to good.

CHAPTER

20

For the next couple of days Matt and the Denver lawmen were constantly on the prowl for Nick Dawson, but they didn't have any luck and that was discouraging. But then, as Matt was coming out of a café after having his midday meal, he spied a huge man with his right arm in a sling lumbering down the opposite side of the street. If he'd not been such a giant, Matt might not have noticed him, but something clicked in his mind, causing him to stop and stare.

It was Cody, Flora's bouncer and bartender!

Matt dodged between several wagons, nearly getting run down in the street by the heavy traffic. With excitement building, he fell into step a few dozen yards behind the giant, certain that he'd be led to wherever Nick was hiding. They entered a seedy neighborhood where it was unsafe to be alone at night and the giant finally ducked into a disreputable-looking saloon called the Rusty Bucket.

Matt considered going to get the help of Marshal Mingus and at least one of his deputies but then rejected the idea. By the time they returned, Cody might be gone. So he pulled his hat down low over his eyes and entered the saloon, trying to be inconspicuous, which was always difficult for a man his size. The Rusty Bucket was a typical low-class drinking and gambling den, but since it was still early in the day, there weren't many customers. Matt stood just inside the doorway, letting his eyes adjust to the dimness, then spotted Cody sitting with an older man near the back of the room.

Matt ducked back outside, feeling sure that he had not been seen. He quickly went around to the rear alley and a back entrance. He tried the door but it was locked, so he put his shoulder against it and pushed hard until the door protested under his weight. It still would not open. That left him no alternative but to just march into the saloon and . . . and what? He couldn't arrest Cody because he was no longer a lawman and he couldn't abide the idea of leaving the man even for a few minutes to get Marshal Mingus or a Denver deputy in order to make a legal arrest. This inability to take action without legal authority filled him with helpless anger.

Matt was still trying to decide what to do when Cody barged outside, practically running into him. For an instant they stared into each other's eyes and then Cody tried to whirl and run back inside, but Matt tackled him. With one arm out of commission, Cody didn't have a chance, and after taking three sledgehammer blows to the face, the giant cried, "Stop! No more!"

Matt climbed off of him and drew his borrowed Navy

Colt. He started to pull Cody to his feet but a motion caught his eye and he saw a man reaching for a derringer. It was the same man that Cody had been talking to in the back of the room, and both he and Matt fired at almost the same instant. The derringer's slug parted hair over Matt's left ear but Matt's Colt drove a slug into the fellow's chest, knocking him over backward.

"Everyone freeze!" Matt shouted, pulling Cody close to use as a shield.

"You shot and killed Mr. Hawk!" the bartender cried in outrage.

"He drew first," Matt said, dragging the giant out on the boardwalk, then forcing him along toward the marshal's office, still several blocks away.

Cody was in awful pain. "Take it easy, I got a broken shoulder, damn you!"

"If you don't move faster, you're going to have a broken skull!"

Matt glanced back over his shoulder and saw the bartender and several customers rush out of the Rusty Bucket with guns. But when he stopped, raised his own weapon, and took aim, they dived back inside.

"Where is Nick?" Matt demanded as he propelled the giant down the boardwalk, scattering people in their wake. "Where is he!"

"I don't know what you're talking about!"

"Tell me."

"No!"

When they came to an opening between two buildings, Matt hurled the giant into the gap and tripped him to land on his wounded shoulder. Cody howled in pain. "Dillon, you're killin' me!"

Matt cocked back the hammer of the Navy and placed

it between Cody's eyes. "I'm going to count to three, and if you don't tell me where Nick is hiding, I swear I'll kill you and claim it was self-defense."

The giant's eyes grew round and he stammered, "You . . . you wouldn't!"

"One. Two—"

"All right! Nick is holed up at the Elkhorn Hotel!"

"Where is that?"

"Just up the street, right at the first block, and you'll see it on the left."

Matt uncocked the hammer of the old black powder pistol and dragged Cody to his feet. "We're going to pay a visit to the marshal's office and then you're going to tell us everything we need to know."

"I ain't killed nobody! Honest."

"Then you've nothing to worry about . . . if you co-operate," Matt told the big man as he shoved him back onto the boardwalk. "But if you don't, you'll be sent to prison."

"They can do that in Colorado?"

"You bet they can," Matt lied.

Minutes later Cody was in a cell and bleeding heavily from his reopened shoulder wound. "You got to find me a doctor!"

"We will," Mingus answered, "as soon as you tell Marshal Dillon whatever he wants to know."

Cody had tears in his eyes. "You'd really let me bleed to death?"

No one said a word in reply. Cody sniffled and his eyes burned with hatred when he looked at Matt. "I just wanted one last try at you. One last try!"

"Sorry it didn't work out. Why don't you tell us

everything you know and save yourself some prison time?''

Cody studied their grim and resolute faces. ''If I tell, Flora will hire someone to hunt me down.''

''Like she hired you in the past?''

''No. I . . . I rough people up to make them pay gambling debts. But I never killed anyone for Flora.''

''But Moses Parker and Charlie Roe killed for Flora, didn't they?''

''Yeah,'' he whispered, unwilling to meet their eyes.

Matt turned to the Denver marshal. ''Get a paper and pen. We're going to get a signed confession that I can use to put Flora in prison for the rest of her life . . . if she doesn't swing.''

After that, Cody confessed what the Dodge City murders were all about and finished by saying, ''Nick was the one that stuffed that apple core down old man Dawson's throat. He said he enjoyed it, too.''

Matt looked at Mingus and the others. ''You all heard that, right?''

They nodded and Matt said, ''I'd appreciate it if you'd take care of that signed confession for me.''

''Where are you going?'' Mingus asked.

''To arrest Nick.''

''I'd better come along.''

''Suit yourself,'' Matt told him as they went out the door and headed for the Elkhorn Hotel.

''Oh,'' Matt said, ''I shot and killed someone named Hawk.''

''I assume it was in self-defense?''

''It was.''

''Then good riddance. The man was nothing but a slick criminal that broke every law he could without getting caught. I've been trying to nail him for years. You show up and do it in a couple of days. Congratulations and thanks!''

Matt didn't feel that any congratulations were in order. He'd killed a man because he'd had no choice, but he sure didn't feel good about it.

The Elkhorn Hotel was a dilapidated two-story brick structure that had survived the fires that periodically swept through Denver. Matt went in the front door and Mingus went in the back just in case Nick attempted to escape.

''Need a room?'' the sleepy-looking desk clerk asked, looking up from his newspaper with a cigarette dangling from his thin, bloodless lips.

''I need to know which room Nick Dawson is in,'' Matt replied.

''We don't have anyone registered here by that name.''

Matt quickly described Nick and ended up by saying, ''He's unwell. Maybe has the plague.''

The cigarette slipped from the slack lips and spilled onto the newspaper, momentarily setting it on fire. ''The plague!''

''I said maybe. But if I were you, I wouldn't want him to die in one of my rooms, because then I'd pity the man who had to clean or stay in it next.''

''Room fourteen. Upstairs. Fourth door on the right.''

Mingus appeared. He looked at the clerk and then at Matt. ''Is Nick here?''

''Yes. Room fourteen.''

''I'd better go in first after him,'' Mingus suggested. ''I'm the law here and you've already overstepped yourself a mite.''

Matt wasn't pleased but he did understand. "I'll be right behind you, Marshal. Just be aware that Nick is very quick and deadly. He knows he'll hang if brought to trial and won't hesitate to shoot it out."

"Thanks for the warning."

"Say, is it the *black plague,* or what?" the ashen-faced clerk stammered.

"I'm no doctor," Matt told him, "so I really can't answer that question. Sorry."

"I'm quitting!"

Matt started for the stairs after Mingus as the desk clerk grabbed his bowler and then left on the run. The stairs were worn and squeaky but Matt figured that Nick wouldn't be alerted because he'd have no idea that he had been tracked to Denver. They halted outside room fourteen and listened for several seconds and then Mingus drew his gun, indicating to Matt that he should try to open the door and then step aside. But the door was locked.

"I'll get it open," Matt whispered, rearing back on one leg and then kicking it with all his might. The door was torn half off its hinges but did not open completely, so they lost a vital moment of surprise as Matt slammed into it with his shoulder, tearing it free and falling into the room as gunfire split the air.

Mingus grunted and staggered back into the hall and Matt raised his gun and fired three times into Nick's chest, stitching it full of bullet holes. Knowing that Nick was dead, Matt jumped up and ran to the Denver marshal's side. "How bad are you hit?"

"Not bad . . . I hope," Mingus said through clenched teeth.

Matt pulled open the marshal's shirt and saw the bullet hole oozing blood from his upper arm. "You'll live," he announced with relief.

"What about your fugitive murderer?"

"He won't."

Mingus was bleeding heavily, so they tied a bandanna around the wound and Matt helped him downstairs. "Where's your best doctor?"

"About four blocks up the next street."

"Then we'll borrow a horse and get there in a hurry," Matt said, leading the marshal over to the hitch rail, untying a stout roan mare, and then helping him into a saddle before climbing up to ride double.

"Good Gawd, Dillon. You come to Denver," Mingus gritted as they started to ride, "you kill two men and wound another and now you're stealing a horse! No wonder you got fired!"

It was a joke and one that brought a tight smile to Matt's lips as he reined the horse around and sent it galloping up the street toward the doctor's office.

Matt was the talk of Denver that day and for many more to come. He sent a hurried wire to Festus advising him to arrest Flora for murder and to wire travel funds even if he had to borrow it from Doc or Kitty, then reluctantly agreed to be interviewed by both the *Denver Gazette* and the *Rocky Mountain News* about the Dodge City witnesses murder case.

The money arrived the following morning and Matt wasted no time in saying good-bye to Marshal Mingus and his deputies.

"I wish I could say hurry back," Mingus drawled with a straight face. "But I don't think me or my men could stand any more of your brand of excitement."

Matt mounted his horse, thinking how he'd need to find and arrest Eddie Porter, Slade, and his partners for assault and theft when he returned to Dodge City. It was a job that he was looking forward to doing . . . with or without a badge.

"I'll be back someday and you'll always be welcome in Dodge," Matt replied as he tipped his hat not only to the marshal but to a large crowd and then touched spurs and galloped out of town.

He stopped at the Blake homestead and spent a pleasant evening with Will, Martha Ann, and little Bessie Sue, returning the Navy Colt.

"I hope it served you well," Blake said after a supper of stewed chicken and dumplings.

"It did," Matt replied. "And I'd like to buy that old saddle you loaned me."

"Why sure," Blake said. "Five dollars would be fair. It isn't much of a saddle."

"It will get me back to Dodge City without blisters," Matt replied, knowing he'd leave this family a twenty-dollar gold piece for their help and hospitality. It was because of people like the Blakes that he didn't lose his faith in humanity. They were everyday people who worked hard on their land and tried to raise their children the best way possible. People like the Blakes were the real builders of this country, though they were modest, neither expecting nor receiving much in the way of help or appreciation. They just worked hard from sunup to sundown and quietly tamed the wild land with the blade of their plow and the sweat of their brow.

"I hope you have a quiet time when you get to Dodge City and win your job back, Mr. Dillon," Martha Ann said after supper, when they sat on the small porch and watched a particularly spectacular prairie sundown.

Matt nodded, knowing that his return would not be quiet. He was beginning to wonder if he really even wanted his job back should it be offered by the town council. "I like this Colorado country a lot," he told the family. "It has a big future."

"Then move on over and join us!" Will Blake suggested with a big grin. "There are some wild mining towns in the Rocky Mountains that would love to have a town tamer."

"I'm not sure that I'm up to taming much of anything right now."

"Then what about Denver? Or Pueblo or even Colorado Springs? Those are stable, industrious communities that can only grow and prosper."

"I'm sure you're right."

"What about farming or ranching?" Martha Ann asked, looking at her husband. "Will, perhaps Mr. Dillon needs a complete change."

"Sure! There's lots of free land to be homesteaded yet. It's long hours, poor pay, and—"

"Will," Martha scolded. "You're not exactly setting this life in its best light."

"I'm sorry." Will reached out and touched his wife's cheek, then stroked little Bessie Sue's hair. "As you can see, there are mighty important rewards and plenty of reasons to live out here where it's quiet, safe, and satisfying to know you're building something for your children's future."

"There's a woman that I'm kind of partial to in Dodge," Matt mused aloud as the sun began to slide into the distant Rockies.

"Then you should bring her over to visit!" Martha

Ann said, looking genuinely excited by the prospect. "She might fall in love with this country and beg you to marry and settle around here as our neighbors."

"Say now," Will added, slapping his knee, "why didn't I think of that? It's a great idea!"

Matt bit back a smile. "Well," he said when it was clear a response was being eagerly anticipated, "I'm not sure that Miss Kitty Russell is cut out for homesteading."

"Kitty," Martha Sue said, "that's a pretty name. What does she do?"

"She owns the Long Branch Saloon."

"Oh."

Not much more was said about homesteading that evening but Matt received a warm send-off the following morning and his ride back to Dodge City was uneventful. Even so, he knew that it was the calm before the storm.

CHAPTER

21

It was almost midnight and raining hard when Matt rode into Dodge City and wearily turned his horse loose in an empty stall at the livery. Water was pouring off the old barn but there was a stack of dry hay inside and Matt tossed several generous pitchforkfuls to his exhausted animal after draping his wet saddle, blanket, and bridle over a stall divider. He picked up his rifle and saddlebags, then slogged through the mud across Front Street and came to the marshal's office.

He knocked and heard old Flora screech some muffled obscenity. "Festus! Are you in there!"

"Matthew?" came the sleepy reply.

Festus was fully dressed when he threw open the front door and blinked at Matt. Letting out an uninhibited whoop of joy, he grinned and exclaimed, "Matthew, you sure are a sight for sore eyes!"

"It's nice to be welcomed back. There wasn't much

fanfare when I left this town and that's for certain."

Festus lowered his voice and stepped outside, where their conversation could not be overheard. "I done like you said. Flora is back in jail but Judge Blasdell says that we can't hold her without some real charges and evidence."

"I've got a signed confession from Cody, that big fella I followed to Denver. He's admitted everything to put Flora away for the rest of her life."

"What about Nick?"

"He's not going to hurt anyone ever again."

"You killed him?"

"Yes, but not before he wounded the marshal of Denver. I felt pretty bad about that, even though it wasn't a serious injury."

"Flora's gonna go crazy when she learns Nick is dead. She keeps tellin' me how her son is gonna come back here and kill me then take over the Dawson Ranch because he's the rightful heir."

"This might send her over the edge into insanity," Matt agreed, pushing past Festus and going inside. He threw off his wet rain slicker and hat, then went over to the cell. "Flora?"

"It's you! I was a-hopin' that my boy killed you by now!"

"I'm sure that you were," Matt told her, realizing he dreaded what he was about to say next. "But I killed your son instead."

Flora's bloodshot eyes bugged. She staggered, then grabbed the cell bars and shook them, screaming, "Liar!"

"Call me what you want," Matt replied. "But Cody has confessed everything and so we can prove you are an accomplice to murder. Flora, I doubt we can get you hanged, but you're going to prison for the rest of your miserable life.''

The woman broke down completely, falling to the floor, screeching like a demented demon.

''You'll get no pity from me or the judge,'' Matt said. ''You've been behind the murders of some fine men, including poor young James Dawson, who never did a thing to deserve being ambushed. In fact, once this gets out, I expect that Marshal Haggen and I will have our hands full just trying to keep you out of the hands of a lynch mob.''

Matt returned to his desk. ''I see you've been saving up my mail, Festus.''

''I sure have!'' Festus seemed glad to turn his attention from the wailing woman. ''Matthew, I already told the town council that I was quittin' this job as soon as we figured out what to do with Flora. I can't take this anymore. Everyone is after me for somethin', or complainin' or . . . oh, it's just been awful!''

''Have you ever been to Colorado?'' Matt asked quietly.

''Why sure, but what's that got to do with any of this?''

''Nothing, I guess. Except that I was beaten and robbed by five men. One is named Eddie Porter. We arrested him some years back. He and a fella called Slade and three others invited me to eat and sleep in their camp and then jumped me at dawn.''

''I can see you been through hell, all right.''

''They said that they were coming to Dodge City.''

''Oh, I did see five rough-looking fellas come, but they only stayed one night. Got real drunk, busted up the Lucky Dice Saloon, and hurt a couple of fellas pretty bad. They passed out in their room. I woke 'em up early the next morning and told them to move on out of town or I'd toss 'em in jail for disturbing the peace.''

"And they went?"

"Sure did!" Festus winked. " 'Course, I had my gun on 'em when I rousted 'em out of bed. And I kept my gun on 'em till they was gone.''

"You did well. They were very dangerous."

"You want me to go and bring 'em back for ya?"

"No," Matt told him. "But if they ever return to Dodge City, I'll remember their faces and they'll be arrested.''

"What about your badge, Matthew? I ain't foolin' none! I'm quittin' if I can't be your deputy again.''

"I don't blame you. I'll talk to our newspaper editor in the morning and he can write up a story explaining everything. That way, nobody has to fear being murdered anymore and I think things will settle down.''

"You're gonna be a hero when everyone learns what you did in Denver.''

"That's the last thing I want."

"They're gonna beg you to pin on your badge. Will you?"

"I might, if I get a good enough raise."

Festus grinned. "What about your old friend Deputy Haggen? Reckon he could get a raise, too?"

Matt clamped a hand on his Festus's shoulder. "If they really want to rehire me, I'll guarantee you'll also get a nice raise.''

"And if they don't agree?"

"Then I'll be askin' you and Miss Kitty to take a

good look at Colorado with me. Maybe even a home-stead."

"Homestead! Matthew, we'd plumb starve ourselves on a homestead! That's terrible hard work and Miss Kitty, well, she ain't made for that kind of livin'. No, sir!"

Matt yawned and headed for the door, saying, "I guess you're right. And you sure did yourself proud here while I was gone."

Festus swelled up like a toad and showed all his teeth as Matt shuffled out the door, saying, "Good night, *Marshal* Haggen."

Festus did a double take, then started to object. "Now, Matthew, I ain't—"

But Matt Dillon closed the door, shutting off his pro-test, and headed back out into the rain toward the Long Branch Saloon, hoping to get a whiskey and a good look at Miss Kitty.

PENGUIN PUTNAM

————————————— online

Your Internet gateway to a virtual
environment with hundreds of entertaining
and enlightening books from
Penguin Putnam Inc.

While you're there, get the latest buzz on
the best authors and books around—
Tom Clancy, Patricia Cornwell, W.E.B. Griffin,
Nora Roberts, William Gibson, Robin Cook,
Brian Jacques, Catherine Coulter,
Stephen King, Jacquelyn Mitchard,
and many more!

Penguin Putnam Online is located at
http://www.penguinputnam.com

• •

PENGUIN PUTNAM NEWS

Every month you'll get an inside look at our
upcoming books and new features on our site.
This is an ongoing effort to provide you
with the most interesting and up-to-date
information about our books and authors.

Subscribe to Penguin Putnam News at
http://www.penguinputnam.com/ClubPPI